HERO OF HER HEART

HERO OF HER HEART

By:

MICHELE WALLACE CAMPANELLI

ARPress LLC
45 Dan Road Suite 5
Canton MA 02021
Hotline: 1(888) 821-0229
Fax: 1(508) 545-7580

Ordering Information:
Quantity sales. Special discounts are available on quantity purchases by corporations, associations, and others. For details, contact the publisher at the address above.

Printed in the United States of America.

ISBN-13: Softcover   979-8-89330-176-2
          Hardcover   979-8-89330-178-6
          eBook   979-8-89330-177-9

Library of Congress Control Number: 2024901792

DEDICATION

This book is dedicated in memory of Jonathan Frederick Gilpatrick. November 26, 1962-March 30, 1995

Contents

ACKNOWLEDGEMENTS

I would like to thank God, my late husband Louis V. Campanelli III, my brother David & Greg, Dawn & Ben, Jonathan "Jono" Gilpatrick's entire family & friends, Melisa & Dick for all their support. To God be the glory!

A special thanks goes to my mother, Fontaine M. Wallace, who raised me to be imaginative and believe in my talents.

Love is patient, love is kind. It does not envy, it does not boast, it is not proud. It does not dishonor others, it is not self-seeking, it is not easily angered, it keeps no record of wrongs. Love does not delight in evil but rejoices with the truth. It always protects, always trusts, always hopes, always perseveres. Love never fails.

1 Corinthians 13: 4-8

PROLOGUE

earching for shelter form the bitter New York cold, the girl knew if she didn't find warmth tonight, she would surely freeze to death.

She approached a man in the park. He was hooded, wearing a long, black raincoat and umbrella. His face appeared friendly, honest. Around his neck, she recognized the universal sign of Christianity, a crucifix. "Sir, would you know of any place where I might be able to stay out of the storm tonight?"

The man looked her over. "Follow me, and I will give you shelter."

Angel followed the elderly man to Rachael's Hotel where he led her to a room with a bed. Suspecting the price to be more than she could pay, Angel turned to leave.

"Wait!" He snatched her fragile arm. "It is not what it seems." Their eyes locked. "You will die if you try to sleep in the streets tonight. It's so cold out there. Just come inside, warm yourself."

Having no job or living relatives, the girl mumbled, "All right." She knew her choices were either follow the stranger, freeze to death, or return to the horrors she had left in the foster home.

The man released her arm and unlocked the door. "God bless you, Angel." He handed her a golden key and walked away.

He knows my name? Angel wondered.

The hotel door suddenly swung open; in the doorway was a man so handsome he took her breath away. He was older than she. She guessed early thirties. His skin was tan. His hair was black as midnight, combed tightly and pulled back into a ponytail. He was about a foot taller than Angel. Muscles pulled his dark trousers tight. His shirt was a sparkling white, buttoned. On top lay a satin white vest, clinging to the sides of his chest. His eyes were as brown as his skin, and he had high cheek bones, a solid stone jaw. He was class with a capital "C," right down to his white gloves and black patent shoes.

"Angel," his voice thick with an Italian accent said, "I am glad you were found."

She straightened her shoulders, tightened her gaze on the man. "You were looking for me?"

"Yes, for all of my life." He reached for her rain-soaked hand, pulled her inside, and closed the hotel door. "My name is Valentino."

He crossed in front of her and seated himself on a plush fabric chair next to the bed. "I was an acquaintance of your father. We met on my estate in Italy. He played me a tape of you singing, Angel. I was quite taken by you, and he asked me to help your career. I couldn't refuse. However, days after, your mother and father were killed in that plane crash, I wasn't sure if I should come. Only recently did I find out how you've been living. I had no idea. I assumed you would stay under the care of a family member."

The girl panicked instantly. "I won't go back to that foster home! Nothing you say can make me! They beat me there!"

"Shhhh," he raised a gloved hand, "you are nearly eighteen now." She blinked and took a deep breath, trying to hide the tears that were threatening to fall.

"I would never take you where you don't want to go. That is a promise." His smile bewitched her. "Don't cry, Principessa, I've only come to give you a job."

"A job?" Hope, mixed with desperation, made her voice waver.

"What do you think about being a professional singer?"

Angel almost laughed. She hadn't taken a bath in days. She was dripping wet, shivering from the cold, and a stranger had come out of nowhere, wanting to give her a job as a singer?

"Angel… Principessa." He rose and came inches from her; his eyes were level with the shiny bronze buttons on his vest. "I believe you can change the world with that unique voice of yours."

"Am I even good?"

"You are a superior vocalist with an amazing vocal range." He slipped one hand into his pants pocket and pulled out a handful of bills, hundred-dollar bills stacked as thick as a deck of cards. "Take this. All you have to do is show up tomorrow at the recording studio, and I'll double it for only a few hours of singing. I'll even let you stay here tonight, as part of the bargain."

"I don't understand."

"You will." He pivoted gracefully and in two strides took the doorknob in hand. With a gentlemanly bow, he exited, leaving Angel bewildered and full of unanswered questions.

CHAPTER 1

Four years later…

The beautiful young woman swerved her car around the last curve in the road, not expecting to find a massive animal appearing out of nowhere.

The tires screeched as she hit the brakes.

The woman screamed, knowing it was too late.

The impact sent the air bag exploding. The bull was knocked onto the hood, crushing it, but not before one long horn pierced the windshield. Glass shards scattered. Blood covered her view of the sky. Hunks of flesh spilled into the seat next to hers, but she was not coherent enough to know if they were from the animal or bits of her own body. Smoke filled her lungs, and the woman faded into blackness.

* * * *

Jono Haze witnessed the horrific accident from the top of the overlooking hill. He coaxed his brown stallion, Wildshot, down to the bottom and into the pool of blood by the car.

Quickly, the large cowboy vaulted from his saddle and walked to the driver's side, afraid of the horrors he might see. He had never seen anyone dead before, nor did he have any desire to. It was his fault, his longhorn that barreled into the car. He felt utter remorse and responsibility for not fixing the broken fence earlier in the morning.

He pried open the car door and began tilting back the brunette head of the woman in front of him. There was no blood on her, only the passenger's seat. His heart raced with hope.

The female's head fell toward him. She was the loveliest creature he had ever seen. He gazed in appreciation of her ivory flesh, delicate features, tiny distinctive cheek bones, full parted red lips and long, black eyelashes which seemed to sweep to the heavens. He could not believe this vision! Even the hair that flowed down her back in long raven curls smelled like his favorite—strawberries! How could one woman contain so much angelic beauty?

Jono had to touch her to see if she was real. "Are you all right, Ma'am?" His large hand skimmed over her white dress and touched her cheek. It was so soft, even softer than a newborn filly's coat.

Slowly, Angel's eyes fluttered open. Beside her stood a pair of enormous legs, covered in dirty, dusty overalls. A large hand that smelled like cow dung was touching her cheek. Immediately, she pushed it away and crinkled her nose.

"Oh, I'm sorry," she heard a male drawl. "I was muckin' out the stalls."

Angel ignored what she could of the stranger for a moment as she began to feel and test her stiff body parts. She tightened every muscle, first her hand, legs, arms, then neck. Nothing seemed broken.

"Do you want me to take you to a doctor, Ma'am?"

A shadow fell across her entire frame, and she glanced up. She could not see him. Her vision was blocked by the roof, car door, and the sun behind him.

"Ma'am, you need to rest." Jono continued to steal her attention away from the grotesque cattle organs lying in the seat next to her. "I can take you to my ranch."

"I've got to call my Agent." Her voice was so shaky she hardly recognized it.

"I've got a phone in my barn. It's not that far from here." A large hand came down to aid her out of the automobile. "Come on."

She grasped the hand as hard as she could and with his help, lifted herself out of the car. Instantly, dizziness came upon her, but somehow, she managed to stand without leaning her frame on his, or falling down.

"Maybe I should take you to a doctor first."

"No, just to your phone." She stumbled back, shell-shocked by the enormous size of the man helping her. A giant, he was, with broad shoulders, scruffy face and a golden lightning bolt earring that hung just below his spiked, blondish-brown hair.

"Are you sure you don't want me to go for help?" he asked politely.

She shook her head no, and he began pulling her over to the stallion. It was the largest stallion she had ever seen, bulky and tan with a long black mane.

"My ranch is right down the road." In a flash, he swung himself up on the leather saddle, leaned his massive frame over and grasped Angel by the waist, lifting her up and plopping her down in front of him as if she weighed nothing but a feather. "Don't fret. I'll make sure Wildshot gives you an easy ride."

She was speechless; amazed by his immeasurable size, strength, and also that he touched her in such an unrefined manner. He had placed a hand on her side, and the other on the reins in front of her, encircling her in arms the width of boulders. She squinted back and up over her shoulder to find the biggest blue eyes staring back.

They were not intimidating, nor frightening. Angel had always been good at measuring a trustworthy person. When she glimpsed the golden cross hanging around his neck, she became more confident. Perhaps he was just a large man on an oversized horse trying to help her.

"I won this stallion at the county rodeo and trained him myself. He may look big, but he's gentle." His blue eyes were twinkling handsomely as he spoke, and she wondered what the rest of his features must look like underneath all the scruffy, unshaven hair.

Imagining, she felt a small twinge in the depths of her stomach. Anger and fear seared through her, afraid of even thinking such a thing. "Stop staring at me, Sir; it's extremely rude!"

"Sorry."

By his stunned expression, she could tell he wasn't used to being spoken to in such a short manner. She guessed, because of his large size and wild appearance, many men wouldn't challenge him, let alone a single woman.

"Well, then stop it!"

"I don't think I can stop lookin' at you." His slick muscles touched her back. His scruffy face tickled her neck as he spoke. "You're about the prettiest thing I've ever seen."

She immediately shrugged him back with a shoulder. "Move away from me! I don't care what you think. And if you try to get that close to me again, Sir, you better have life insurance!" Jono leaned back in the saddle in disbelief. Did she actually just push him? He moved closer to check.

A feminine elbow went for his ribs but missed.

"It's nice to know you're gainin' your strength back." He admired her character. "My name's Jono Haze."

The smelly hand on her waist, Angel noticed, was leaving large amounts of dirt on her Marinna dress. "That's a nice name."

"Yes, Ma'am, it is. You're welcome to use it." He snapped the horse's reins and they continued the journey down the open dirt trail leading to a wooden ranch house barely visible in the distance.

As they drew closer, Angel began to feel the atmosphere around her sinking in. The land was absolutely beautiful and peaceful. Golden-green grass rolling as far as the eye could see, swaying in the breeze. Fat tan cattle, dozens upon dozens, were grazing on a hill and on the grasslands below; wasting time lazily, as the sun began setting behind them. There were no sounds of beeping automobiles or the bustle of city life, only loud moos, crows cawing, and the whistle of the wind rustling through the grass.

There is calmness, openness here, she thought. *Instead of tall buildings and airplanes, this place is a sanctuary; where man and nature live together as one, with a subtle, inviting ease.*

The house, coming closer, was wooden and painted white. It was two stories and had an added enclosed screened-in porch and a picket white fence. A garden of sunflowers grew in front with corn, tomatoes and other plants Angel didn't recognize. Hanging in the windows were potted plants, some with tiny African violets. White curtains blew in the wind. And clothing dangled on a clothesline on the side of the house where Jono halted Wildshot. It was all so quaint, well-kept and welcoming; not at all what she had expected this big, rugged man to take her to.

Behind the house, in the golden field was a larger red wooden building, possibly the barn he was referring to. It was long and stuck out in contrast to the cool yellow-green colors of the grasses. Above the door, read a sign in big white lettering, HAZE RANCH. A horse with a rider wearing a large cowboy hat was entering the building.

"Who is that?"

"One of my ranch hands."

"You own all this land?"

He smiled. "Yes, but I share the house with my grandmother." Jono leaped off the high horse and waited to see if she would be able to get down on her own. When Angel finally realized what he was waiting for, it was already too late. His dirty enormous hands were on her, slowly, gently, pulling her down. Their bodies collided; woman on man, feminine softness against hardness, molding together only for an instant, but it was fire on fire.

Her feet touched the ground; immediately, she pushed him away, stepping back, puzzled by the emotions coming over her.

"Skinny thing! Boy, maybe you should take her out back and feed her like you did that filly this morn'."

Angel's eyes turned toward the woman's voice coming from the screened-in porch and she gasped. An older woman in her mid-to-late seventies was seated in a wheelchair. She had a striking resemblance to Angel's own mother who had been killed in a plane crash when she was only a young girl. Her hair was the same color, shoulder length and black with white streaks. Her aged face even was as attractive and comely in a slightly different way. She had large eyes, like Jono's; with the sunlight, she couldn't tell their color.

"Where's your manners? Tell her to come in and sit a spell with this ol' lady." The woman patted a rocking chair next to her wheelchair for Angel to come join her on the porch.

Angel walked toward her in an incoherent gaze, flooded with wonderful memories of her own mother greeting her with the same becoming smile.

"What's your name, Deary?" Her black eyes twinkled. "You'll have to forgive my grandson's manners. He doesn't meet city folk out here."

"Angel Frederick."

Her eyes widened for a moment as if she recognized the name. "I'm Mrs. Grace Haze."

Angel noticed the picture on her lap along with a knitting needle and quilt. Inside the frame was a photo of a Native American man with long gray braids.

"And this is my late husband." Mrs. Haze gladly explained the picture on her lap. "I keep this with me as a good luck charm."

Angel saw the love in her eyes for the handsome man in the photo. She obviously missed him very deeply.

"How do you feel?" Jono crossed in front of his grandmother and leaned his massive frame down low to hand Angel a glass of water.

"Much better." She observed the concern in his big blue eyes. "Thank you." She watched him through lowered lashes as she took a swallow and placed the glass on the rocking chair arm.

"Well now, that's more like it—manners."

Jono's cheeks, even through his facial stubble, were turning a crimson shade of red. With a brief nod to Angel, he retreated into the house, embarrassed.

"Would you like to stay for dinner? Jono's a wonderful cook."

"I'm not sure. I need to make a phone call."

"Well, go ahead and use our phone." She smiled. "I'll get my grandson to show you where it is." And her hand enclosed Angel's, holding it.

Angel instantly liked this woman. She was drawn to her loving, caring nature, and reminded Angel of her mother whom she'd thought forgotten. Angel wanted to reach out and thank her for bringing back those long-lost treasured memories.

"Jono, Angel needs the phone."

"Your name is Angel?" Jono appeared in the doorway and leaned a bulky shoulder on the frame.

"She sure looks like an Angel, pretty as Mother Mary herself." Now it was Angel's turn to blush.

Jono witnessed the reddening of her cheeks and relished having made such an effect on her. Frankly, the prospect surprised him. "Come on, I'll take you out to the barn."

Angel rose from the rocking chair, waved goodbye to Mrs. Haze, and followed the enormous man outside and onto the golden grass.

"My grandmother has taken a liking to you," he commented as they walked around the house to the large red barn in the field.

The wind ruffled Angel's hair. She was suddenly conscious of her body- hugging white dress as she strolled beside him.

Jono wanted to tell her he was beginning to like her, but guessed a woman like this would think him crazy for spouting how he felt after only knowing her a few minutes.

"Looks like it's going to rain." Angel's attention was drawn up into the blackening clouds that were blocking the last of the sunset.

Jono couldn't care less about the storm coming right now. Angel was the first person besides his family to not cower away from him. Madison citizens, for the most part, walked on the opposite side of the road when he and Wildshot passed. No one talked freely to him. Even his ranch hands tried their best to avoid him as much as possible. Unless there was trouble—then he was the first they or the town called upon.

"So, why is your mother in a wheelchair—or is it none of my business?"

"She fell downstairs at my mother's house." He would tell her anything she wanted to know. "Her Doctor doesn't predict her ever walking again. But my grandmother says she's waitin' until God tells her that."

"Your family believes in God?"

"Of course." He cocked a brown eyebrow. "Don't you?"

"I suppose I do. My mother used to read me the Bible when she was alive and take me to church."

"My grandmother reads the Bible every day." His voice was muffled as they reached the open barn door.

Inside were several stalls, all containing horses of various sizes. Light shone through the knots in the red wood, making it possible to see to the very back of the long barn where there was a chair in the corner. Placed on top of it was an old-fashioned rotary phone. To the right, and above, was a rusty showerhead spigot. *One,* Angel thought, *Jono should use right about now.*

"There it is."

"Thank you." Angel took a step toward it. "I need privacy." Then she went to the receiver and dialed her band's Agent number in New York. In the background, she heard Jono's thunderous footsteps exiting the barn.

Someone answered the line. "Brannett Entertainment Agency, World Wide, New York Division, this is Mindy. How may I…"

"Mindy, get Eric Brannett on the phone. This is an emergency!" The call was immediately transferred.

"Angel!" Eric Brannett sounded frantic. "I have been waiting for your call. Valen has been in a rampage ever since he's discovered you were late for the band's cover shoot!"

"Eric, I was in an accident near the 196 exit."

"Are you all right?"

"Yes, there's a ranch down a dirt road almost parallel to where the rent-a-car was hit. I'm not hurt, but please, send someone to come and pick me up."

After he briefed her about her boyfriend, Valentino, being so worried he had called every police station and hospital in El Paso and Madison County, Eric Brannett informed her the *Rock-N-Country Magazine* shoot had been rescheduled.

"Why? I can make it now!"

"The famous cowboy your band was supposed to meet to teach you how to ride refused to come. It seems the wind knocked down some of his fences. He couldn't even make it to lend you his horse or meet their reporters. And there's a tornado warning out for all El Paso. The shoot has to be rescheduled for some time next week."

Angel's heart sank. *Another week, another week to do the photo opportunity of a lifetime! A week is an eternity!*

"Eric, I can do the magazine cover. Call them back and explain why I was held up."

"Don't you worry about that now, Angel. It's more important that you find shelter and stay there. Are you safe? Are you alone? Whose ranch is it?"

"I'm with a bunch of hee-haw's, okay? One of them hasn't bathed in a year. Now you call *Rock–N-Country* back! No, one second, thought have Valen call *Rock-N-Country* from the Milan office."

"Valen, isn't in Italy anymore."

Angel heard a crunch behind her. She whirled around to find that Jono hadn't completely exited the barn. He had been eavesdropping, standing in the barn's doorway all this time! What would he do or say? She'd just blatantly insulted him.

She gawked at his enormous build, the engorged muscles bulging from his arms. He appeared more like an animal than a man since he was so dirty. His face, however, did not show even a hint of anger. She decided to trust her first instincts. She had sensed he would not hurt her. And his earlier concern had shown her as much.

"I'm going to wash up a bit and then get started on your dinner as soon as I know what you would like to eat."

She had been right. She breathed a deep breath, relieved. "Chicken will be just fine. I really don't care for…" She stopped herself before she admitted she didn't like beef. He was a cattle rancher, she realized.

"Chicken, it'll be." Jono gave her a rugged smile and left, his shoulder looking as broad as the doorway.

"Angel, listen to me. Are you there?"

"Yes, I'm still here." She placed the receiver back to her ear.

"You must stay there until the storm passes. Is that clear? I'll contact *Rock-N-Country* tomorrow or as soon as we're able to send someone." Thunder shook the barn, startling her. The call was dropped. Outside, darkness was engulfing the sky; clouds as black as midnight were rolling in, swallowing what was left of the sun's rays. The wind was picking up speed. Lightning seemed to be flashing, right, left, everywhere across the sky.

Angel hated storms, hated them when they turned this severe. The hail rains and strong chilly winds always reminded her of being caught out in dangerous storms when she ran away from her foster home. Ever since Valen had come into her life, she always believed she would never be alone to face another deadly storm again. But now she was here, and he was millions of miles away!

She loathed the feeling coming over here; the sudden fear gripping her heart and stealing her breath away, the sudden helplessness that seemed to consume her sanity. This anxiety always overwhelmingly made her want to run, anywhere.

So she did. She ran into the golden-green fields, unprotected, to reach the two-story in the distance. Angel did not want to be alone; she wanted to have the solid house around her if a tornado did come.

Halfway to the house, a gust of wind knocked her clear off her feet. Her knees sank into the grass, and she let out a bloodcurdling scream.

Jono, hearing her cry, rushed like the wind to be at her side. His enormous arms wrapped themselves around the frightened woman. He lifted her and hurried toward the house.

After setting her down, he shut the door behind them. Instantly, he reached for her shaking hands. "Are you okay?"

She felt foolish.

He observed her flushed face, fluttering lowered lashes, and tried quickly to make her feel unashamed. "That was some wind. It scared a lot of critters, not just you."

Angel released his large hands and shook the rain off her dress. It was covered with yellow grass stains and ruined. She turned her back to him.

"Don't worry about being scared. It's okay." Light from the lightning lit up the house and he saw her back muscles constrict. "This house, I built myself and it's strong. I'm strong. We'll help protect you from the storm."

She smiled to him over a shoulder, realizing he was only trying to make her feel better. Surprisingly, his presence was putting her more at ease. So many times on the streets she'd been alone, but not tonight. Jono was with her, just like Valen would be if he were here.

"So, are you married, Angel?" Mrs. Haze inquired, wheeling herself into the living room.

That was not a question Angel enjoyed answering. "No."

"Good, then they'll be no questions. Tonight, you stay with us." She stopped rolling next to a sofa and beckoned Angel to sit next to her with a pat of her hand. "There's an extra room upstairs, a guest room across from Jono's. I insist you stay until the storm passes."

"Thank you, Mrs. Haze." Angel wiped the back of her dress to make certain she would not soil the sofa then she sat down and studied her new surroundings.

The house was indeed lovely and as sturdy as Jono had announced. Leafy potted plants were in every corner. Pictures hung on the wooden walls of Mrs. Haze, her husband, and of many children. The furniture was handsomely carved out of wood, stained a dark red to match the wooden walls and floors. Pillows of white and blue were on the sofa, matching the white curtains, giving the home a country feel. The kitchen was open and connected to the living room. Stairs to one side of the kitchen ascended to an upper level. A hallway was to her right.

The roof seemed strong enough. Rain could barely be heard with the windows locked. A fine enough place, as Jono had said, to stay out of the storm and try to feel safe.

Mrs. Haze noticed that Angel had been searching for the room. "Are you nervous about something, Deary? Is there something I can get you?"

"She'll be fine," Jono protectively cut in.

"Yes, I just don't like storms. It was a storm like this that caused my parents' plane crash," Angel admitted. "I also just heard that the photo shoot I've waited a lifetime to get, just got rescheduled. It isn't my day, I guess."

"Nonsense, you met us, didn't you?" He grinned with his face beaming.

"Yes, I did." Angel returned the smile.

"Maybe your shoot wasn't meant to happen today." Jono walked to the kitchen and began preparing dinner. "Everything happens for a reason."

"That's right," Mrs. Haze agreed, her dark eyes dashing back and forth. "You know, once when I was even younger than you are now, I knew a dog. Oh, what was his name? Duff… no, his name was Duke."

"Grandma, she doesn't want to hear your stories." Jono shoved a pan of chicken and biscuits in the oven.

"No, it's fine." Angel glanced at him. "I love stories."

"Yes, women like to reminisce, Son, don't you know that? Maybe, I should tell her about the time your sister Nikky stole your clothes from the pond and you had to come home naked."

Jono shook his head. "I think I'll be taking my leave now."

His smile was blinding. Mrs. Haze pressed further. "That will be fine. Women-folk want to discuss women things, you see."

Jono winked at Angel lightheartedly, then walked up the stairs; his feet pounded against the wood. "By all means, then, please excuse me."

When he turned, disappearing at the top of the stairs, Angel felt a disturbing loss. The realization frightened her. She knew it wasn't because she was still in need of his comforting presence, for her nerves were returning back to their normal relaxed state. And it wasn't because she minded listening to Mrs. Haze's stories, for she honestly couldn't think of a better way to pass the time than talking to this caring woman. No, it was simply because she wanted him there.

"Oh, he's just jealous. He wishes he could be the first to tell you about Duke."

"Well, I think you should tell me about that dog. He was yours, wasn't he?

"No." Mrs. Haze blushed. "Actually, I know far more interesting stories if you'd like to hear them. These stories would really upset my grandson if he knew I was telling them."

"What stories are those?"

"The 'Cowboy' legends."

"The 'Cowboy.'" Angel's eyes brightened. "You know of him?"

"Of course, where do you think the legends come from?"

"You're kidding?"

"No." Mrs. Haze grinned. "The 'Cowboy' lives in this part of El Paso County, right here in Madison."

"Do you know him personally?"

"Yes, Deary."

"I've read so many stories about him. I wanted to actually meet him before my photo shoot, but he called and cancelled with my Agent."

"The 'Cowboy' is a very busy man, saving so many lives."

Angel took a deep breath. "Is everything I've read about him true? Is he really a hero?"

"So many times over, I can't even count. He's like a Saint!"

Angel smiled. "Isn't he just a normal man who happens to be at the right place at all the wrong times?"

"Maybe, but not every man would be able to do the things he does." Angel patted her hand.

"That's true, Mrs. Haze."

Mrs. Haze's eyes suddenly began to tear. "You know, Deary, I'm so glad I've met you. It's so nice having someone to talk to."

"I'm enjoying your company too, Mrs. Haze."

"Can I tell you a secret? The 'Cowboy' isn't everything the paper says. He's a hero all right, but he's not very happy."

Angel bit her lip. "He's not?"

"No, you see, because of his heroic efforts to save others, he has in a sense killed off his own self."

"I don't understand."

"Well, it all started when he was only fourteen. I remember every detail of him riding into Madison for a social gathering among the townspeople. It was a birthday party for young Jenny. That's when he became known not only as a hero but a vicious fighter."

"A fighter?"

"You see, in order to save Jenny he had to kill a mountain lion, the largest one ever recorded in these parts."

"How did he kill him?"

A tear rolled down Mrs. Haze's cheek. "With his bare hands, Deary."

Watching Mrs. Haze cry, her hands trembling in her lap, Angel instantly realized this story was too painful for her to talk about. "If this is too upsetting a story to tell, Mrs. Haze, please tell me another."

"It's all right."

Mrs. Haze grew silent for a few minutes while she wiped away her tears and tried to contain her sorry.

"He was just going to Jenny's birthday party. He didn't wish for Jenny to run off the porch, away from everyone."

"No, of course not."

"You see, the mountain lion rushed out of the bushes, leaped through their family's barbed-wire fence and charged right for her in front of everyone in Madison."

"I read about this!"

"Yes, this rescue made all the headlines. But, please, don't think that just because he killed that mountain lion he's a heartless animal-hating man, because he's not," Mrs. Haze insisted. "He had first ordered his horse to jump the fence to try to lead the mountain lion away from the girl. His horse can outrun anything."

Angel watched as more tears gathered in the corners of her dark eyes. "I didn't think anything like that, Mrs. Haze. I think he is a very brave man."

"He is." Mrs. Haze's voice cracked. "Not many men would have tried to save little Jenny at all."

"Not with their own lives in danger."

A moment passed. Angel leaned further back into the sofa. "No one but him could have saved Jenny and been able to live through it."

"It wasn't easy. His horse bucked him right off instead of helping, right in front of the beast. He had no choice but to tackle and wrestle the mountain lion down to the ground." Mrs. Haze closed her eyes. "The mountain lion kept fighting, and fighting, kicking, and thrashing his claws about. That boy finally was forced to try and knock the mountain lion out with a mighty punch between the eyes. Unfortunately, it was a fatal blow; he didn't know his own strength then."

Angel threw back her aching shoulders. "Can I ask you a question?"

"Anything."

"Why does telling this story make you cry so?"

"He is blessed, or cursed now, depends on how you see it, Deary. After that day, people forgot that his biggest strength wasn't his muscles but his heart. They forgot he was just a human being. All people seemed to care about was how many pounds he could lift, or how many people he's saved over the years." Mrs. Haze reached out her hand again and took Angel's gently. "Promise me something, Deary, when you meet him and know who he is, you'll treat him with respect."

"Of course."

"He's a wonderful man with a big heart. He would never hurt you."

"What's his name?"

Mrs. Haze laughed. "Don't you know it's supposed to bring bad luck when you speak his name?"

"Oh, that's just superstition, right?" Angel asked. "That's why the newspapers won't print his real name, only 'Cowboy'."

"No, the newspapers won't print his real name because it sells more papers to have some hero running around like Batman."

"Well I have to admit, every time I see 'The Cowboy' Saves Again," I buy," Angel said.

"Yes, most do. That's why they keep up this charade." Mrs. Haze sighed. "Then, of course, we have the local townspeople believing if you say his real name and he finds out, he won't save you in time of trouble."

Angel asked, "So what is his real name?"

"Don't tell her." Jono slowly descended the staircase and chills radiated down Angel's spine and to her very core watching the dark, rugged, masculine man reenter the room. All thoughts of the cowboy legend disappeared. Jono had bathed and changed. He was bare to the waist. His massive muscular chest was still moist with tiny water droplets. Only his golden cross hung down between his broad shoulder blades to the top of one nipple, crowning his physique gloriously. His jeans clung so tightly to his flesh she could see every rippling long muscle. The jeans were torn slightly at the knees, but they were the brightest of blue and smelled like heaven compared to the dirty overalls he had been wearing. He looked so different, clean, so handsome and mysterious. It took twenty of Angel's pounding heartbeats for her to remember that he was not a dream, that in fact he was real and standing just across the room.

Every inch of her being wanted to leap off the sofa, run into his arms and feel the rippling muscles tighten around her.

She never imagined this was possible, that it would happen again. That indeed she would find another man other than Valen attractive.

She tried to pry her gaze away from his body, but the feat seemed impossible. If only he didn't look so perfect and hadn't tried so hard to get to know her! He had rescued her from the car accident and storm.

He hadn't even raised his voice when she had thrown her elbow at him on the horse ride here. No, what was keeping her eyes locked on him was much more than what her eyes could see. Jono was a compassionate, understanding man who was already becoming her friend.

Her gaze rose and found his big blue pools staring back, filled with such kindness. Immediately, the warning voice in her head screamed for her to listen. *Look down, for goodness sake. Don't let him know you find him this alluring. Valen is your boyfriend. This man who came out of nowhere with a body chiseled out of stone is only mere temptation. Temptation isn't love; it must be dismissed and simply overlooked! You must not think otherwise. He is nothing more than a sweet hunk of man flesh. Valen is the one who owns your heart. Look away, damn it, look away!*

Angel turned her eyes to the wooden floor and straightened her dress still weathered by the storm.

"I didn't think you'd mind me telling her who the 'Cowboy' is."

Jono scratched the bottom of his chin with a slight smile as if it didn't bother him. "You talk too much about the so-called legend." He moved into the kitchen, turning his back to the both of them.

"I do not!" Mrs. Haze claimed.

"Lying's a sin."

Mrs. Haze humphed. "I was just going to tell her who he is."

Jono turned and shook his head at his grandmother. When Angel's gaze moved toward his grandmother, Mrs. Haze changed the subject.

"My Son, those biscuits smell great. Are they done?" Jono walked over to check.

"Oh, Jono makes the best meals in all Madison. He does everything great, takes care of this big house, ranch, even mucks out the stalls when Billy's sick. He doesn't have to do that, but he does. I'm very proud of my grandson. Someday, he'll make a woman a fine husband, a real fine husband."

Her meaningful boast was obvious and Jono must have heard his grandmother from the kitchen. Immediately, he pulled the pan of biscuits out of the oven, along with the honey-baked chicken. "Dinner's ready."

Angel rose and followed Mrs. Haze to the wooden kitchen table not more than twenty feet away. There was a space for her wheelchair to fit right under. Angel sat on her right while Jono began setting three plates of biscuits, chicken and fresh out-of-the-garden corn on the table. When finished, he sat across from both of them.

"Jono, I think it's your turn to say grace." Mrs. Haze clasped her spotted hands into a praying position. "Please, do the honors."

He folded his large callous hands, plopped his elbows on the table and closed his big eyes. "Thou prepares a table for me and my cup overflows. Amen."

"Amen," Mrs. Haze smiled brilliantly. "Now, what's that, Son?"

"Psalm 23." He stuffed a biscuit into his mouth, engulfing it in one bite and devouring it down in two giant gulps.

"Psalm 23:5." Then Mrs. Haze turned to Angel before beginning to eat herself. "But he's not that great with numbers."

"Who could memorize all those numbers like you?" Jono ripped off the skin of a chicken breast and swallowed half of the visible white meaty portion. "Knowledge must only get better with age." The topping of honey on the meat smeared across his lips and he quickly wiped it away with the back of his hand.

Mrs. Haze huffed, hiding a smirk. "Well at least I have the decency to wear a shirt to the table and eat with a fork every now and again."

Angel chuckled but quickly stopped as soon as she witnessed Jono lifting one of his eyebrows, watching her.

"Would you like me to throw on a shirt, Angel?"

Never. "I suppose I can ignore your chest."

"I like to eat chicken with my fingers. Does that bother you?"

"I eat barbeque chicken with fingers all the time." She smiled. His eating habits were the last thing on her mind after the chest question which enabled her to glance at his muscles briefly.

"Good." And he chomped down another hunk of white meat with a nod. "I want you to feel at home."

I do. "Yes, thank you."

"No, thank you for being our guest," Mrs. Haze blurted between bites of her biscuit covered with melted creamy butter. "It's nice to see someone else for a change around here."

With a loud thunderous bang that shook the windows, the lights suddenly flickered and then went out completely. Angel let out a gasp. She had completely forgotten that the storm was still raging outside. She clutched her chest as fear came back—fear of the storm, the darkness losing in on her.

"Are you finding the candles for us, Son?"

Worry made her eyes squint. It was impossible to see if Jono was searching for the candles in the blackness. She prayed he was. Jono was her only hope to find those candles since she didn't know where anything was. She heard him stumble then she saw a match being lit, his hands carrying candles quickly back to her.

Jono placed two in the center of the table, lit the candles, and sat back down in his seat. "You okay, Angel?"

"Yes, I'm fine." And she was, as soon as she met his comforting gaze. His eyes were calming, full of concern, full of adoration.

Mrs. Haze glanced over to the two ogling each other, and coughed. "Know what, Son? I'm feeling a bit tired. I need some rest. Save some dinner for me for tomorrow."

Jono broke off his gaze to watch his grandmother wheel away through the living room and down the hallway.

"Good night, Angel." She waved. "See you in the morning."

"Good night, Mrs. Haze. Thank you for letting me stay during the storm." But as soon as Angel thanked her, she was truly wondering about Mrs. Haze's intentions. Was Mrs. Haze really tired and in need of rest, or did she just want to leave her alone with Jono in the candlelight?

CHAPTER 2

"So, what do you do for a living, Angel?" Jono questioned, drawing her attention away from his mother leaving.

"I'm a professional singer. I have a solo album and also sing in a band."

"A singer, I should have known with that sweet voice of yours." He observed her for a moment longer, then spoke. "Is something bothering you?"

"No." She picked up a biscuit and snipped off a small proportionate bite. The piece melted in her mouth, but she wasn't the slightest bit hungry.

"You're not scared to be alone with me, are you?"

"No." She wondered why she was so attracted to Jono when she already was involved with one of the most desirable business men in the world, Valentino.

"Then you're not hungry?"

She didn't want to hurt his feelings by not eating the meal he had prepared. "I'm sorry. Maybe I just need some fresh air." She rose and headed for the porch. She needed to sort through her conflicting thoughts and emotions.

Distancing herself seemed to be the only answer, but Jono was soon at her side.

"Here." He had a blanket in his hand. "Don't get sick out here." His big blue eyes showed such tenderness. "It's getting chilly."

Angel sat down in the rocking chair farthest from the screening which was still dry and took the blanket from him.

He gave a forced smile. "Are you sure that you're okay?"

"I'm fine."

"Are you positive you don't want me to take you to a doctor?"

Angel couldn't believe men like this existed. "Thank you, Jono, but I'm fine."

"You wouldn't lie to me, would you?" He bent over, putting his hands on his knees to look deeply into her eyes.

"No." She smiled.

"Good, I try never to lie."

He was captivating. His every move was solid, confident and masculine. Angel was drawn to him. He was so close! She wanted to reach out and grab him. She wanted to know what it felt like to have him wrapped in her arms.

She couldn't stop herself from moving closer to him. Angel felt as if she was being pulled by invisible strings. Subconsciously, her body arched upward. His full masculine frame was closing in. Just yesterday, she knew where her life was headed and now… and now… Angel snapped her body backwards. "Was that your bull that ran into my car?"

Jono stood abruptly. "Don't be upset with me. I'm willing to pay for all your damages."

She felt horrible that she sounded angry with him when all she wanted was to stop them from making a terrible mistake. "You don't have to pay for damages. It's a rental, but I just wanted to know."

"Property is property. I respect others and then they'll respect mine. That's all there is to it. I want things right between us."

"Jono, I…"

He leaned close, again. "Can you forgive me?"

She knew she couldn't win this argument. "Yes, of course, I forgive you."

Jono winked goodbye to her and walked back into the house through the open doorway.

Outside, clutching the blanket, she hid from the wind. Angel felt her guilt fading. Really, why should she still feel guilty when she hadn't even kissed him! Why should she feel horrible about being attracted to him? Women are attracted to men every day without acting upon it. Jono was just a new friend, a friend that she would never see again once Eric Brannett sent a car for her.

That's the way it had to be and would be.

As she rocked, watching the Colorado night storm, she remembered the reason why.

* * * *

Two years ago, on the night of her twenty-second birthday, Angel had almost cried herself to sleep. Valen had left her. Her dreams had been destroyed. What was being famous, when the man she wanted to marry refused her! She had waited years since Valen took her off the streets, too many years. And now that she was older, Valen had broken off their relationship because of, "reasons."

"What reasons?" She banged her fists into her pillow. At that time, she didn't know. Valen would not reveal his reasoning, only that she would never see him again.

Didn't Valen love her? If he didn't, maybe she should find someone who would! She decided to go to a local dance club to get her mind off Valentino's breaking up with her and not to spend her twenty-second birthday brooding alone. Why should she care if Valen didn't love her anymore or want her as his wife? There were other men who might.

At least, that's what Angel told herself.

At one o'clock in the morning she strolled onto the local dance floor at the Powerstation, strutting through the sweating dancers. The lights were flashing colors of red, green, and blue around the room. The beat of the bass was pounding the walls and floor. It made her want to dance the way young virgins shouldn't.

Her dress fit her like a second skin, tight and red, clinging. The neckline plunged to her stomach exposing, accentuating the swell of her large bosom, and skinny stomach. The dress was very short, only hanging to her upper thighs. Her red high heels were five inches tall, designed to seduce any man as she sashayed across the floor as only Angel Frederick the Star could.

Her eyes searched through the dancers for a partner. She wanted a man, any man that might want her enough to at least help her forget Valen's last rejecting words, "I cannot love you as you wish, Principessa. I am no longer yours."

Angel had almost given up, no man came close to Valentino's class and decorum until her gaze met a man's leaning against the back wall. Nearly six feet tall, he had solid, defined muscles and short white-blond hair. He was tanned, dark and slender. Girls surrounded him, eight of them, and none of them could hold a candle to Angel.

The blond, he was her target.

A clear path opened in front of him. Angel took this opportunity to dance like she did during her music videos. Men seemed to like that.

She began to sway her hips, to the right, to the left, lower, glancing over her shoulder at him. Swinging her buttocks, thrashing her hair, Angel danced dirty to the beat that was driving her with an animal lust for sexual intoxication.

Male eyes were on her from everywhere, but there was only one man she wanted. Only one she wanted to gain the affection of, to make her forget Valentino.

It was all for the stranger with the short blond hair.

The man's gaze was piercing through her skin. Angel felt his want and beckoned him with her body; she felt him come up behind her, sweat dripping off his body onto hers below. He wanted her.

They danced, beyond comprehension, their passion multiplying, responding with unstopped abandon. Her back was against his chest and his hands were in front of her trying to touch her curves through her clothing. Their bodies rubbed and caressed one another's; the desire for untamed, unbridled sex building to the sounds of the club's music, to the drums and bass.

Angel couldn't take it anymore. His erotic, masculine scent was closing around her. The slow thrusts of his pelvis through their clothes made her ravenous. She had never known desires of the flesh before tonight, and she wanted to learn.

She had waited for Valen for years, waited for his marriage proposal and for their blissful wedding night. But that night was never meant to be. Valen had broken off their relationship. Valen being her husband someday was never meant to be.

Angel whirled around on her tippy toes, and kissed the blond man hard against his lips. His tongue slipped into her mouth and intertwined with hers in a frenzy. Angel lost herself; the room was spinning.

Who was this man? Who was the stranger with the blond hair? "You're very sexy," he whispered into her ear.

"Then call me that again," Angel said.

"My name's Jack, Sexy."

She looked into his hazel eyes, saw his want for her, his inclinations. "Take me home, if I can please you, Jack."

CHAPTER 3

Angel and Jack entered the small hotel room, kissing gently on the lips. "Undress in the bathroom," Jack said, "while I fix up the bed a bit."

"Oh." She felt her cheeks get warm.

"You're a very beautiful woman, Sexy." His mouth curved into a smile revealing a deep dimple in his lower left cheek. "I am so honored."

"I'm…" She wanted to explain what her life was like, the reasons why she couldn't date anyone until she was sure Valen was forever out of her life, but how? "I'm…"

"…in a relationship." Jack finished her sentence. She turned suddenly pale and still.

"What's wrong, Sexy? You look like I've upset you."

Angel crossed her arms in front of her chest. "I'm sorry if I've givenyou the wrong impression. I wanted to kiss you more, but I didn't realize that you wanted a serious relationship. I'm going out of town for a few months, but maybe then, we could get together for a date."

"There is no reason to make stuff up to me," Jack said. "Are you going back to Italy, to Valen?"

Angel almost fainted. Her heart seemed to stop beating. *He knows!* Jack knew she was dating Valen!

"I know that Valen broke up with you," Jack announced matter-of- factly. "I work for him, security guard, Fourth Division."

"I see." Angel gulped.

"I was assigned to keep watch over you until Valen returns from Italy to talk to you."

"To talk." Angel ran into the bathroom, slammed the door and locked it.

He tried to open the door, nearly ripping off the handle. "Please, don't be angry. Open up."

Angel sank to the floor, tears flowing down her cheeks. "You should have told me you knew Valen before I ever kissed you."

"Please open this door!"

She felt so ashamed. Valen wanted to speak to her again? She'd kissed one of his employees on the very night he broke up with her. All hope of fixing their relationship was destroyed!

"Let me explain. I was trying to get you out of that club. I knew Valen wanted to talk to you again and I didn't want you to make a mistake. Valen may be my boss, but he doesn't own me!"

"If I am crazy to have let you kiss me, to have taken that risk being one of his guards, then I'll pay the price!" Jack said. "You don't know how some men can act in those clubs, Sexy. I was doing what I needed to protect you and get you out of there."

There was a long silent pause before Angel decided to crack open the bathroom door. It took every ounce of her willpower to walk out. She drew herself up bravely and faced him. Jack stood towering over her. There was empathy in his eyes, not anger.

"You're right. I should have told you I was one of his employees," Jack said. "Then you kissed me and I seemed to forget for a little while."

This was too much for Angel to comprehend. She began to cry, half hating Jack, half appreciating what he'd done. Did he really care for her?

"For so many years I've been loyal to Valentino as a guard."

"Valen told me that he hires many men to guard his house and his offices worldwide."

"You're never to know we are there," Jack explained. "If you figured out we were there then our cover would be blown."

He suddenly reached out and pulled her into his arms. "So, you were told to watch me."

Jack laughed. "I'm his worst enemy, if the truth be known, having to watch how he treats you. He orders people around like dogs. All he cares about is money and connections. He thinks because he's rich, he owns everyone. Money can't buy the way I feel about you. It can't buy what I felt when I kissed you. The feelings we shared were mutual; you can't honestly say that you weren't attracted to me, too."

"Please, stop talking like that."

"Like, we should start dating and have a life other than being owned by Valentino? He took you as a child mourning her parents and made you into his dependent, not the woman he wants to marry."

"That's not true."

"If you only knew what I have learned over the past few weeks. You don't even know what… what he does!"

Angel glanced up through her tears. "You hate Valen and want to hurt him, through me!"

"Stop being so loyal." Jack instantly put a finger to her lips, hushing her. "I have had feelings for you for quite some time now. I've watched you grow into a stunning woman from that scared little teenager." Jack pushed a strand of curly raven hair out of the pool of tears on her cheek. "Do you know how many times I've been ordered to keep an eye out on you? I've seen how many times you cried over how he won't ask you to marry him. Every time you wept, it broke my heart. I am the one who has fallen for you."

"But I love him."

"No, you don't. You can't!"

Angel shivered in his tight hold. "If you've seen me cry, then you know I do."

"Run away with me. I'll protect you from him. I know the other guards, and they will look the other way."

She gasped. "You are betraying his trust."

"No more than you just did." Jack dismissed his actions.

"Dancing with you was a mistake, probably the biggest mistake of my life! I do love Valen! If he wants to talk to me then maybe he wants me back. I never want to see you again for as long as I live. You took advantage of my trust. The thought of you watching me makes me sick! Aaaagh!"

"I risked my life telling you all that you now know. I've waited years to talk to you."

"You don't give a damn about me, or you'd know that I love Valen. You should have told me that he wanted to talk to me before you kissed me. You used me for some kind of personal revenge because you don't like my boyfriend." She threw her hands to her waist. "You got your notch on your belt, now leave me alone."

He interrupted her fit with a clenched jaw, speaking through his teeth. "Then why did you bother to try to seduce me?"

"I thought that Valen was done with me."

"You are still a child."

Angel wiped her drying tears and headed for the door. She didn't want to hurt Jack. She did care for him. But it was for his own good. She couldn't let Jack continue risking his life to want to be with her. If they started dating, and Valen found out, it would not be pretty at all.

"You do not love him!" Jack shouted as her hand grabbed the doorknob. "Out of all those guys, you picked me to kiss. You should be glad it was me!"

"I'm sorry."

"Angel, whether you believe me or not, I love you. I'm a better man than Valen. I must save you from going back to that monster. Even he knows he's a monster. Why else do you think he broke off your relationship in the first place?"

"Stop it! Stop it! Stop talking about Valen that way." Angel couldn't hear another word. She tried to run past him, but his arm snaked around her stomach. She almost lost her breath, he squeezed her so tightly.

"Do you know why he's coming back to talk to you?"

"Tell me what you think then."

"He's planned your wedding, Angel; you and him in Hawaii on the fourth."

"What?" She couldn't believe what she was hearing.

"That's right. He missed you so much he's planned your wedding." Jack's face showed his disapproval. "Did he even ask you? No, of course not! He owns you. He doesn't want to ask. He does what he wants, when he wants."

"I can't believe it."

"In that sick head of yours that probably even makes you happy. You finally will be wed to Valentino. A ring, however, does not make a man treat you right."

Angel clutched the hem of her dress in despair, utterly confused. Valen missed her! He'd planned their wedding while she was planning to make love to… "No!" How could she live with herself? Valen still loved her, and she'd almost given away her virginity to another man.

"If you do love Valen, you wouldn't have danced with me the way you just did. Not the way we were, Angel, not how wonderful we were together." Jack wrapped his arms around her once more, leaned down and kissed her gently on the cheek. "You don't hate me; it's impossible."

She had to forget she ever met Jack. She was going to marry Valen. Angel glared downwards, bit her lower lip, and gripped her hands together until her knuckles turned white. Then, she said unemotionally, "Kissing you and our dancing at the club meant nothing. I am Valen's. It never happened."

"You can't mean that."

Tears fell down her cheeks. She glanced up to meet his eyes and they were in agony. She turned away, facing the opened door. She didn't know what to do. She had never seen a man cry over her before. Lord, Jack was crying… over her.

"Valen has never taken you into his heart. Valen doesn't know how to love, not the way love can be. Damn you, you're so blind; caring isn't love."

Angel grabbed her purse from off the bed, wiped the tears off her face and headed toward the door.

"I have never felt for anyone the way I do about you, Angel."

Such a powerful and attractive man, so brokenhearted over her. The sight of him was almost too much to bear. Part of Angel wanted to run to him, another wanted to run as far away as she possibly could. She had to listen to his words, even though it hurt. Jack deserved that much. He had risked everything to tell her what he had.

"I have never wanted to be with a woman more than you. I will never forget what it was like to have you in my arms. I'm going to save you from him. I know that you're only trying to protect me, and that's why you are being cruel. But I knew what I was getting into when Valen hired me." Jack placed his hand over his heart. "I will somehow show you what real love is, if it is the last thing I ever do."

Angel was about to break down and admit that when she kissed him, she thought she felt something, too. Instead, she ran out the door before she lost the courage to run.

* * * *

Jack never did show her what real love was; Angel remembered, rocking in the chair on the Hazes' porch. He never lived to see another day.

CHAPTER 4

"Hi," Angel said, staring up at the shirtless cowboy wearing nothing more than a pair of jeans and a cowboy hat.

"Hey," he said and offered back a smile.

"Thank you, Jono, for bringing me to your home and introducing me to your wonderful grandmother. I might have been stuck in that car for hours if it wasn't for your help."

"You're welcome."

"Your ranch is so beautiful, even in the rain."

"Even in bad weather?"

She blushed. "I only get scared of tornado storms when I'm alone." Her gaze drifted down his six-pack stomach.

"Your bedroom is upstairs, second door on the left when you are ready. Breakfast is at dawn."

"I'm not tired yet."

"Stay out on the porch as long as you like," Jono said.

Angel continued to rock. "I won't be much longer. I promise. Would you care to join me?" She invited him to sit in the rocking chair next to hers.

"The last time I sat in one of those chairs, I broke it." Angel laughed.

Jono smiled. "Those chairs are precious to my grandmother. My grandfather made them. She likes to wheel herself out here and talk gossip with the ranch hands."

Angel watched a lightning bolt flicker in the sky. "You two must get along well with your employees."

Jono leaned against the wall beside her and crossed his muscular arms. "Besides my family and a few others, I keep mostly to myself."

"I'm sure everyone likes you."

He raised a brow. "You're a lady. Maybe, I'm just extra nice to you."

"You didn't even raise your voice when I insulted you in the barn earlier. Most men would have."

"I'm not most men."

"Most men wouldn't have forgiven me for being so rude and you…"

"…have." Their gazes locked "You were just stressin'." She grinned.

"You've got a pretty smile."

Her long eyelashes fluttered as she fought the urge to blush.

"A lady who looks like you must have a boyfriend or a husband." She was glad he inquired.

"Yes, a boyfriend."

"You've probably got a lot of friends, too."

"None that could have helped me the way you did today," she said.

He moved closer. The lightning bolts shining in the sky were reflecting in his blue eyes. "You're a friend to me now."

"Yes, of course." Her palms were beginning to sweat having his body so close to hers.

"My friends are welcome on my ranch. Any time you feel like visiting, please do. Remember that."

Angel couldn't take her eyes off of his handsome face. "I will."

"Promise me, Angel?"

"I promise."

Jono straightened. "I'll see you later, then. Someone's coming for you now." He turned and walked away without saying goodbye.

"Jono, what do you mean?" She raised herself from the rocking chair, but a noise stopped her from following.

The noise was coming from the direction of the storm, coming toward the house. She scrunched her eyes and recognized instantly the dark sleek outline driving down the dirt path heading toward her. Eric Brannett had sent a limousine for her. She will be able to leave.

She waved her hand to the driver, lifted her finger to have him wait a minute, then she hurried back inside the house. She had to say farewell to the man who had helped her so much.

Jono was nowhere to be found. A light was creeping down from up above, through the red grooves in the wooden ceiling. He must have gone upstairs! She ran up the steps, one by one, and discovered the lights were only coming from an empty room. But across the hall another light was seeping through the bottom of a closed door. Could that be Jono's room?

Angel wanted with all her heart to knock on his door and stay in his room. She wished she was a free woman. A woman who could snuggle into Jono's boulder-like arms, fall in love and tell him exactly how attractive she found him. She hadn't ever felt this way, not even for Jack. She longed to tell Jono. Oh, what reckless thinking!

One man was already dead because of her selfish lust, Angel reminded herself. She couldn't possibly feel for anyone except Valen. Angel had learned her lesson. She accepted her fate: Valen must be the only man in her future now.

"Goodbye," she whispered, her hand still on the closed door. "I'll never forget your kindness, Jono."

Jono heard her from the other side.

Angel rushed down the flight of stairs, through the porch and to the back of the limousine where the driver was running over to open the door.

It swung open before the driver got the chance. A large masculine hand suddenly snatched her waist and yanked her down into the limousine and into a pair of coat-covered arms. Angel was squashed against a silk gray shirt. She recognized the smell of his musk. Angel shivered realizing who was holding her.

Only one man moved with such style, dressed with such immaculate precision and smelled of the finest cologne. Valen, himself, had come for her.

"Are you all right, Principessa?" Valen embraced her. "Eric never mentioned you'd have to drive alone. What the bloody hell was he thinking?"

"I'm fine, Valen, really."

"Nothing like this will ever happen again!"

He put his hands on her cheeks, forcing her lips inches from his. His eyes dances like smoldering embers. Brown as his skin, his eyes glistened with want and anger. "I will not have you traipsing around alone. Think of what could have happened."

"Nothing happened to me. I'm fine."

His lips swooned down and captured hers. She complied, passively opening her lips to aid his tongue in entering her mouth.

He broke their kiss "Oh, I've missed you, Principessa."

She leaned her head against his broad shoulder. "Prove it, Valen. You said that if we got back together, we would eventually get married. Yet, you still haven't asked me or discussed a date."

Before another plea finished leaving her mouth, his arms fell to his sides, and he turned toward the window. In stony silence, he glared out into the summer rain.

Angel tried to fight off the tears, but they still came, as did a knot in her throat. The feeling, common, too common to her, again returned with Valen's utter rejection of commitment to their relationship.

His hand lowered slowly and covered hers. His gaze never left the window and what was beyond. "We shall wait."

How many more years must she wait? When would they marry? She wanted to shout those questions from the highest mountain, screaming at the top of her lungs.

She took a deep breath while his fingers entwined with hers and she saw his hands. They were uncovered today when normally he wore white satin gloves. Immediately, her anger vanished.

The first time she had seen his hands, she nearly got sick from the sight. The second time, she cried. Today was the third. Today, she felt pity. Scars of his past were cut deeply into his hands, burns on his fingers, lacerations on his knuckles. His pinky finger on his left hand had been ripped open and badly sewn back together. Blister prints were still visible on his right hand.

How could he not be so cold with a history like his own? A past, Angel wished she could not feel just by holding his hand or see just by a simple removing of his gloves.

"I'm sorry for asking again. I didn't mean to upset you." Angel peered upward from his hands to the vast emptiness on his face as he stared into the Colorado storm.

"It's all right, Principessa. I love you."

She wiped away her tears, deciding that there was no point in continuing crying to make Valen feel guilty for not marrying her. She already knew he loved her. Trust was the issue, after he learned about her almost-encounter with Jack. Angel straightened her shoulders and tightened her upper lip. "So where are we going?"

"New York." He gave a smile to ease the mood. "I scheduled you to be on *The Jim Griffin Show*. The taping is tomorrow."

Instantly, she became enthralled. "*The Jim Griffin Show*!"

"I'm glad it pleases you."

Angel wanted to hug him for putting her on one of television's most prestigious talk shows, but she knew Valen would take any thanks from her as an insult. He would hush her thanks, always did. Everything he bought for her, he bought because it was his way of showing her how much he appreciated her. He enjoyed giving her things. He felt it was expected. He felt it was needed.

"I bought a Chenez dress for you in purple. It should make… as you Americans say…the women eat out their hearts." His accent turned into a chuckle. "Your hairdresser will be there as well." "Great," Angel agreed.

"It is very short notice, I know." He pulled her once again to him and kissed her gently on the tip of her nose. "Jim Griffin promised to behave and speak only about your upcoming album."

"You know what's best."

His unreadable expression curved into a smile. Angel felt her blood pressure rise as his hand rubbed against her back.

"Well, I certainly made an error putting Eric in charge of your affairs this week. I can't believe his idiocy at not hiring you a driver. To think what could have happened. You could have been killed in a car accident, or those who found you… they didn't touch you, bloody hell!"

"No!" Angel gulped, trying to contain his sudden fury. "It is a woman staying at the ranch. She is quite pleasant."

His eyes were calculating with doubts. "A woman who owns a ranch that size, living alone?"

"Yes, she lives there with a grandchild, Valen. I suppose she hires cowboys to help her."

"To round 'em up." Valen grinned. "I didn't meet any of them."

"I see." Valen's every word was said with unmistakable, innate grace, but lurking behind was a morbid intensity that made her wary.

"I saw one from a distance."

He shrugged back a shoulder and faced her more comfortably. "Eric told me that one, you had said, hadn't bathed in a year."

"Well, I was just anxious, that's all," Angel admitted through a forced smile.

"I hope she bathes her grandchild, then." Valen tilted his head to one side, cocking it authoritatively.

"I don't think she does. He smelled really horrible. I couldn't even stay in the same room," she said.

"On the ranch it may be normal for them not to bathe every day. In Europe, you know, people don't bathe as often as they do here in the States." Valen glanced back over the land as the limousine turned off the property by way of the dirt path. "Just be thankful you'll never have to worry over such things as paying for water."

"That's true."

He lifted his arm around her, pulling her closer against his chest. Her hands touched the soft fabric of his shirt. "You will never have to run away again or live out on the streets."

"Thanks to you, Valen."

He shifted forward for a glass off the table in front of them and snapped the crystal decanter off its holder. It gleamed with brilliance reflecting a wicked flash of lightning as he filled one glass with wine.

Out of a back pocket in his slacks, Valen lifted out a small white pouch. He put two pills in his mouth, and then added a yellow powdery substance to his wine. Would you like a glass of water?"

"No."

"We've got a long trip on the plane. I need to get some sleep."

Angel regarded the drugged wine apprehensively. "I wish you'd stop taking so much. I don't want anything to happen to you."

Valen chuckled. "Don't worry about me, Principessa. I'm invincible." Then he quickly sipped down all the glass' contents.

"If that were true, Valen, you wouldn't need so many pills all the time."

CHAPTER 5

Valen appeared as handsome as ever, dressed today to the nines in a black and gray lined, tailored suit. The black suited him, as did the satin gloves covering his hands with masculine decorum.

"Are you still tired from the plane trip, Principessa? You seem distracted."

"No, I'm fine." She wasn't, she was nervous and fidgeting.

"Well, you look very lovely this morning."

Her hands clasped tighter in her lap. "Are we late? I would really prefer if we weren't too late."

"Late enough, we're almost there." Valen showed her which building it was by pointing a gloved finger. "It's right around the corner, right here."

Stagehands were already in the street waiting for the limousine as it rolled to a stop in the back entrance of the CSN studios. He saw her flinch and took her petite hand. "Remember, no matter how you do today. I will always love you." Valen kissed her forehead, pulling her into his arms.

"Can you tell I'm frightened?"

"No," he lied. "I just know you well enough to realize you might be. In time, I promise you'll get used to this attention."

"You said that many years ago, and I still get nervous for interviews."

"So I did."

One of the stage hands opened the door, startling her and she jumped. "Miss Frederick, this is…" She didn't catch the name. "He'll take you to your dressing room."

"Thank you." She took the assistant's hand and rose. Valen was at her heels, not taking his brown eyes off the man either.

They were led into a tiny room where Nathan, Angel's favorite hairdresser, was waiting. She gave the young man a nod and sat in the chair across from the lighted mirror.

"I'm waiting in the green room, Principessa." She felt a dress being laid across her lap. "I hope you like it."

Glancing down, she immediately approved of the tight purple satin bodice and the slit on the right side of the lengthy skirt. The neckline was lower than moderate and backless, a little daring for Valentino's contour classic taste, and even more beautiful than expected. It was obvious he had bought the dress for her, so she would like it.

Angel bit her lower lip not to thank him; instead, she shifted straighter in her chair, looked over her left shoulder and uttered, "I love you, Valen. Thank you for thinking of me."

His smile melted her. And she turned her attention to fixing her makeup in the mirror.

She watched him leave in the reflection. Minutes passed and with every second that the hairdresser worked his magic, she felt more and more like a Princess. Her hairdresser was lifting handfuls of her raven hair that fell to her waist, teasing it into a bold exotic fashion. Each curl was mastered into a breathtaking romantic creation.

"You're absolutely the best hairdresser in the world," she praised. No answer. She found his silence unusual. "I'll be sure Valen gives you a bonus for this, Nathan."

His head tilted down and then he began to touch up her makeup as if he hadn't heard her.

Why was he ignoring her? Something must have happened. Her hairdresser wasn't himself today. Angel wanted to inquire why he was acting so strangely, but decided it wasn't her place, nor would Valen approve of her asking him a personal question.

"I don't need any bonus," he finally spoke. "Tell Valen to keep his money. I flew here to help you, not him. This is a big interview for you, and I wanted you to look fabulous."

"Did something happen between you and Valen that I am not aware of?" Angel inquired at once. None of Valen's employees ever seemed to enjoy working for him. To them, Valen was cold, hard-nosed, stubbornly overbearing and aggressive, but normally Nathan was immune to him. "Please tell me what happened; I don't want any problems between you both."

"Don't concern yourself." Nathan grabbed a make-up brush and started blending in some rouge.

"Was it about pay?" She guessed by his earlier statement. "Did Valen disagree with you about your wages?"

"Can I speak to you without Valen learning of our conversation?" Nathan took a quick glance around the small dressing room.

"We're alone."

"Then I'll say only this; Valen is a very difficult man."

"Yes, he is. It's taken me years to care so deeply for him."

"I don't know how you deal with Valen at all!" Nathan winced, knowing he had just stepped out of line.

Angel knew he was only stating his opinion. "I know him better than you."

"I wish you the best, Angel." Nathan added more color to her chin. "I hope this is not the last time I get to do my hair and make-up artistry on you."

"Don't be silly. Valen won't fire you."

"Then I'll quit." He then kissed her on the cheek, surprising her. "Au revoir."

"This isn't goodbye." Angel watched him leave. "Is it?"

Through the years, Angel had been through thousands upon thousands of employees coming and going. Many quit, many moved or changed their lines of work. Because of this constant transience of employees, Angel had given up on trying to make friends with anyone. She'd given up on opening her mouth and begging an employee to stay.

She couldn't' blame them for wanting to quit working for Valen, really. He was a very difficult man to understand, especially when he was on those pills. One moment he could be calm and easy to carry on a conversation with, but the next he could be loud, vicious and on an emotional roller coaster.

It had taken Angel many years of caring for him and understanding his physical and emotional condition for her to accept their way of life.

She had to block out the world and forget her dreams of having the perfect man to achieve this certain little sanctuary in her continuous universe of turmoil.

Valen needed her. He needed her more than any of her dreams of another man, so she stayed by his side and remained loyal. She had to be, she was the only person Valen had ever loved.

Knock! Knock!

"Hold on a minute!" Angel took her time slithering out of her dress and into Valen's exquisite purple gift. She was still nervous about being a guest on Jim Griffin's talk show. "Come in." She walked to the door and opened it for the man calling.

A stagehand entered. "It's time, Miss Frederick."

"Wait a minute. I haven't been briefed. I don't know what kinds of questions Mr. Griffin is going to be asking."

"Just be yourself. Don't be nervous."

She gave him a wary smile. How unusual, she contemplated, no briefing? She trailed behind him, her head held high, her hips swaying inside her purple gown. Her heels were clicking on the hard tile floor, veiling her nervousness.

Within seconds, the audience was spellbound, cheering, clapping as Jim Griffin entered his modern, eclectic-styled set. Angel watched him at the far right of the stage from the sidelines, waiting for her cue.

"Hello, hello, hello," Jim spoke into his microphone without a gray hair out of place. "My guests today are women of divine beauty and fame. You all know who they are. They are women of glamour! Ladies and gentlemen please welcome to the stage, Miss Angel Frederick." He came across the set before the white desk and black chairs.

The stage hand motioned Angel to step out onto the stage and sit on the first chair to the audience's right.

The lights blinded her as she took her first step into the limelight. The cameras were rolling, the people were screaming as she waved hello into the blinding air.

"From the band Black Widow, the one and only Angel." Griffin's announcement only excited the audience further as Angel slowly lowered herself into the chair.

"Good morning, Jim." She pretended to know him well.

"This year has been full of rock star and politician news. Today we're going to discuss the pros and cons of being a famous musician in the upcoming century. Are these ultimate dream girls truly every man's fantasy or are they just stuck-up divas? And do they use their feminine beauty to influence every man surrounding them, even the public at large? We'll discuss if these women are truly as perfect as a picture when the Jim Griffin show continues in two minutes, two seconds."

After the short break, Jim introduced his second guest. "Cheral Richards, everyone!"

Angel was completely dumbfounded. She's on the show? How'd Cheral manage that? Cheral was supposed to be in London! Why did she come here instead of her gig with Bad Girls? What was going on?

She glanced over to the beautiful blonde as she strutted across the floor in tight bellbottoms and a ruffled yellow velvet shirt. Her blond hair was parted down the center and straight. Her lips were painted a brilliant fuchsia to match her platform shoes.

Angel smiled brightly to Cheral in acknowledgement as Cheral seated herself.

"Cheral," Jim Griffin called, posed, leaning against the desk, his arms folded across the chest. "Let's get right to the point of the show." "You are a singer, correct?"

"Yes."

"Then you earn your living by using your voice. How did you land your job in Bad Girls, Cheral?"

"I met my manager while in the grocery store shopping in L.A."

"Isn't it true, Cheral, that your manager was always trying to get you into bed?"

"Excuse me?" Cheral gasped.

That was a rude question; Angel's heart began to pound wondering just what kind of questions Jim Griffin would be asking her next. What kind of show was this? Valen wouldn't have subjected her to this!

"Isn't it a fact, Cheral, that not only was he after you to sleep with him but also half your teachers in college tried as well?"

Cheral sputtered with fury. "So, what if they did hit on me? I never complained."

"Isn't it true that throughout your life your good looks have helped you to get higher grades and better business contracts? That you have slept your way to the top?"

"That is a lie!"

"And, you, Angel Frederick, isn't it true that your singing career was hand-delivered to you by your admirer as well?"

"I have worked very hard for many years to have the opportunities that I have now. I've been doing shows since I was eighteen." Angel interrupted, not knowing how to stop the slander that was coming out of Jim Griffith's mouth. "Having talent is why I have such a career today."

Jim Griffin glared, tugging hard on his white tie. "Did talent, as you say, deliver your career to you, or did one Italian business mogul take you off the streets because of how you looked?"

That hit a nerve, and she began to wilt in the seat.

"Valentino, himself, took you under his wing because he felt pity for the young orphan girl who ran away from a foster home and was living on the streets. He even gave you plastic surgery to make you into a better-looking woman so you would make it in show business!"

"That's not true!" Angel spit out. "I've never had work done."

"Your breasts are not real and we found a doctor who claims that you've had total facial surgery."

"How dare you!" Valen crossed the set fuming to the side of Jim Griffin. He towered over the older man. His eyes were a piercing black fury. The cameras turned instantly for the confrontation of the two men. "How dare you accuse Angel of such a thing? If you have a question about something we've done in the past, ask me, bloody hell! And how dare you lie to me about not starting one of your scandals!"

Jim Griffin began to take a step back. Valen was livid, but Angel knew Griffin wouldn't retreat much farther. He was getting the story of his life, baiting and provoking one of the most famous business men in the world.

"Well, why don't you explain why you took a teenager, a no-name girl, and blackmailed Eric Brannett into being her agent?"

That did it. Valen grasped Griffin's jacket with a clenched fist and raised the other one to swing into a right hook. Suddenly, the punch stopped inches from Griffin's nose and Valen held it, midair, for quite some time, until he began to laugh.

Laugh?

His laughter didn't stop, barreling out deeply from his chest—it was evil, it was pleasant, it was funny.

Angel started to giggle, so did the audience; before long, even the stage hands and audience were clapping.

Valen released his strong grasp and pointed a gloved finger dead center into Griffin's skinny chest. His eyes were dancing over him. "I should have known you were a low enough man to try to hurt the reputation of the woman I love."

Angel's heart eased realizing Valen was coming gallantly to her rescue and he wasn't going to fly off the handle, at least not yet, anyway.

Valen withdrew his finger and threw up his hands. "You see, Audience, there is no story here. I helped Angel because from the first moment I heard her sing, I was mesmerized. I knew exactly what kind of singer she could become, and one of the top agents in the world agreed with me. I aided her, yes a bit, but not with blackmail. Eric Brannett's agency listened to one soundtrack and believed in her talent as much or even more than me."

His head turned to Griffin and he patted his shoulder very hard. "What we have here is a struggling reporter digging up nonsense to smear the name of my girlfriend." His voice darkened. "I will not let him hurt us. Griffin deserves my fist, but I will not drop to his level, at least not on television. I am sorry if I scared anyone." He gave a sexy, debonair smile. "Please forgive me and believe me when I say the only reason I got carried away is because I love this woman with all my heart. I will protect her from any defamation of character," he glared at Griffin, "with all of my being."

Protect Angel like no one had ever protected him. Angel's heart was beating a mile a minute as the audience began to applaud again.

"Now if you will kindly excuse us, we must be going now that we have caused such an unpleasant scene." Valen put his arm around Angel's shoulders gently. They both turned and Valen began to lead her to the edge of the set, to an emergency exit. "Good day." Valen halted when they reached the exit door and swung himself halfway around, his hand on the red door handle, his eyes skimming over the audience.

"Thank you for inviting us on the show, Jim. Thank you for admiring my girlfriend's perfect body which is, by the way, unaltered by surgery. There is nothing wrong with plastic surgery, but Angel has had none as you claimed here today. This show has been an interesting experience, I must say. You'll be hearing from us again, or should I say our lawyers. Yes, mine, Angel's and Brannett's for that matter. *Arrivederci!*"

Valen opened the emergency exit door; the alarm sounded. Jim Griffin's face went pale as Valen then led Angel out into the mid-morning sun and into the hustle of New York City.

CHAPTER 6

Within minutes, the limousine drove through the golden drawbridge at one of the finest restaurants in the world: *Philmores*, a castle reconstruction of Renaissance Gothic architecture of the fifteenth century. The sun's rays were beaming through the main cathedral-styled windows as the high- pointed arches and pinnacles reached heavenward. Its majestic beauty was beyond any king's greatest fantasy, straight from the pages of a fairytale.

"Bloody hell, Griffin's going to pay for trying to degrade you!" Valen promised as the couple emerged from the limousine.

Valen stomped past the allegorical depictions of men and ancient beasts carved in the ivory-arched grand entrance as Angel followed on the red carpet leading into the Courtier Hall.

All servers were standing in a line; all candle chandeliers hanging from the arched ceiling were lighted and giving the palace a romantic, medieval glow.

"I can't believe I was so stupid as to trust the likes of him."

The vein in Valen's left temple had been ticking since they had left the studio. Angel knew not to say a word until he calmed down at least another degree.

An usher approached them with wine-filled goblets set on a sterling silver tray. Valen seized a goblet and threw it across the room. It crashed against the black and gold marble floors and shattered. "I rented out this restaurant to ask… damn… bloody damn the lot of them! I can't enjoy myself now, bloody hell!"

Every server's eye had turned on him during his temper tantrum. Angel gently touched the edge of his black suit jacket and whispered for his ears only, "Please, Valen, let's try to enjoy lunch anyway."

His brown eyes narrowed. "I about fed you to the lions… now it's all wrong… I can't, bloody hell."

Angel blinked away sudden tears of frustration. She had been trying to calm him down now for several minutes. She hated when he became uncontrollable; it frightened her. "Valen, please, you're beginning to make a scene. Why don't we just go back to my apartment and I'll make you something to eat."

He grabbed her chin tightly in his hand and she tore her eyes away in defiance. "If you only knew why I wanted to bring you here, you wouldn't say such things. I can make a damn scene if I will please."

She shuddered but held her ground and he released her. "Valen, just forget about that Griffin show!"

"How can I? I trusted him and he tried to hurt your reputation."

"It wasn't personal, okay? I'm fine. He just wanted to have a sensational show, that's all. I'm not upset. Please, don't you be."

Valen took her arm and led her into the majestic ballroom. Tapestries and oil paintings of the owner's ancestors hung on every lavish golden wall. Her eyes focused on them, not the man who was infuriating her at the moment. Valen placed one of his gloved hands on her back and coaxed her to dance as the lutes began to play Angel's favorite waltz, Tchaikovsky's *Waltz of the Flowers*.

He pulled her closer to him suddenly, like a Prince trying to sweep her off her feet. His love for her was now flowing through his fingertips as their silhouettes flickered against the cathedral decorated walls.

"I lost my temper again." He said this as a statement, not a question. She nodded. "Look at me, Principessa, when I speak to you."

She did, and his brown eyes sparkled when they met hers. "I owe you an apology." Her lips curved into a slight smile.

"That's better." He tightened his hold on her, and they continued to dance into another song. His black hair swirled behind him with every graceful masculine step.

She loved dancing with Valen. Watching his muscular body move to music was the greatest aphrodisiac she had ever known. He danced with such passion.

A server tapped Valen's shoulder, and he stopped at once, catching Angel as she almost tripped into him. He pulled her possessively to his chest, scorning the waiter as he informed them that their first course was ready to be served. Valen only shooed the annoyance away and began to dance again with his Princess.

Several songs passed and then he asked, "Principessa, are you hungry?"

"A little now," she replied.

He lifted her into his arms at once and carried her slowly through the gold-black marble pillars and into the adjoining room of the castle. Her lavender dress cascaded down around his black Italian suit, swirling to the floor and flowing around his ankles. With every step, he gazed deeply into her eyes.

"Have I told you how much light you bring into my darkness, Principessa?"

"No." She blushed.

"You are brighter than the sun." He placed her down tenderly in the private dining room, the garden room. In the center of lush plants, white roses, glorious magnolias, pink rhododendrons and a waterfall, sat their table.

She stared at him. The desire for her was in his brown eyes. Could this be the night? The first night that they would finally make love? Perhaps they should continue to wait until their wedding bed, she pondered.

Valen pulled out her Victorian-styled chair and then he seated himself as he prepared internally to propose. His palms were beginning to sweat, his knees were shaking. "You mean everything to me, my life, my breath, my reason for living. I never told you this before, but over the years, I have purchased many rings in hopes of having the courage to ask." Angel smiled, tears coming to her eyes.

Valen poured wine into their crystal chalices on the table and raised his. "To us, Principessa, the world is ours." She lifted her cup and drank heartily. Her eyes never left his.

"Principessa... I..." The words didn't seem to manage to come out of his mouth. "Never mind, pass the butter." She handed him a butter plate, and he set it down beside the basket of small dinner rolls.

"Damn it," Valen muttered in disgust. "That's not what I wanted to ask. I wanted... bloody hell... how can any man go through this?"

"Go through what?"

"Nothing!" He gulped down more wine.

"Aren't you hungry?" Angel questioned as she took a bite of her roll.

"No." Valen tried to slip out of his chair to drop down on one knee, but his legs didn't seem to want to budge.

"Valen?" She gave a puzzled look. "Is something wrong?"

"I just wanted..." He spilled the wine, knocking the glass over with an accidental bump of his hand moving across the table.

Angel gasped.

"Bloody hell!" He took a spoon and dipped it in his chowder. Raised it halfway to his mouth and saw that she was staring at his shaking hand.

"Valen, are you not feeling well? Is it your hands or your back?" He set the spoon back down into the soup bowl. "What's wrong, you're shaking!"

His chiseled features were tense. He clenched his jaw and shifted his legs underneath the table. "There's something I need to... never mind... your chowder is growing cold!" He placed a hand to his stomach.

"Valen, are you getting sick?"

"No, damn it, eat!"

Angel jumped in her seat from his yell and then took another sip of her soup as if nothing had happened.

"I'm sorry," he muttered, grateful Angel was forgiving by nature. "It's just… I didn't mean to… bloody hell!" Valen reached in his suit jacket and felt the velvet jewelry box through his gloves. "When you were lost somewhere in Colorado, I came to realize just how much I would miss you."

"Oh, Valen." Angel was deeply touched. "I'm fine. Nothing happened."

"No, you're wrong, something very significant happened. You are my whole world, Principessa. I wouldn't want to live without you. If something had happened to you, I—"

She interrupted. "You would have dealt with it and moved on." Tears came to his eyes.

"I couldn't move on."

"Sure you could have. It's what I would want."

"No, I could never move on. I would have regretted with all of my heart not becoming your husband." Valen's voice cracked. "I would have regretted never… bloody hell!"

"Please, stop saying 'bloody hell.' What's wrong, Valen? Tell me."

Valen commanded his shaky hand to bring the box from his pocket and show her exactly why he was so jittery. He hoped with her witnessing the ring, he wouldn't even have to say those words.

"Valen, you're turning pale." He cursed underneath his breath. She lifted a black brow. "Valen?"

His hand inched from his pocket and brought the jewelry box outward to her. "Another present?" Angel's eyes widened with surprise.

Valen's arms were trembling. His fingers went numb and the box fell from his hand into Angel's chowder, causing hot liquid to splatter all over her bosom and the front of her dress.

She let out a scream, snatched the table cloth and began wiping off her chest and dress. Her skin was turning a bright red as if it might blister.

"Bloody hell!" Valen stood up, throwing his napkin on the table. "I try to propose to you, I lose my temper, not once, but twice, throw chowder on you; it's no wonder why you'll say no!" He started taking long, angry strides toward the entrance of the restaurant.

"Wait!" Her scream stopped him, but he didn't turn around.

"Yes, yes, I'll marry you!" Her heels clicked against the marble floor, and then her arms wrapped themselves around him in a loving hug.

CHAPTER 7

Hearing the ring, Angel stumbled out of bed to her night stand and answered her cordless telephone. "Hello."

"Eric Brannett, your agent here. Sorry to wake you."

"What time is it?" Angel slithered underneath the bed covers again and leaned her head back onto the pillow, placing the phone to her ear.

"Nine o'clock in the evening."

"Did I oversleep?"

"No, the concert isn't until tomorrow."

"Oh, that's right." Angel rolled over onto her side, hugging her blankets softly to her bosom. "So why are you calling?"

"Two reasons, one is that Rock-n-Country Magazine has rescheduled." Angel fully awoke.

"So, I'll be returning to Madison, Colorado?"

"Yes, next Monday at ten o'clock in the morning, same location. Your plane leaves at two in the morning, red eye out of LaGuardia."

"That's fantastic!"

"Yes, we're very proud of you at Worldwide. This Magazine promotion will almost guarantee our record sales doubling this year since you are branching out into the country market."

"Yes, it probably will." Her enthusiasm dropped. "Are you upset?"

"I'm sorry," Angel said. "Maybe the business side will grow on me after a few more years."

"How can you not like it? Do you know how many people starve and struggle their whole lives to get the same opportunities you are handed!"

"I just like to sing, Eric. Being my agent and providing me with lack of privacy is your side of the business. So why else did you call? You said there were two reasons." Angel truly despised that her agent didn't fully understand her need for personal time. She'd rather change the subject than discuss it further.

"A package arrived at our office for you today with a return address from Madison, Colorado."

"Really." Angel slipped her legs out of bed with the covers falling to her waist. "Who is it from?"

"Perhaps I should tell Valen about it."

Angel knew the significance of that response. "That isn't necessary. I don't know anyone personally in Colorado."

"Such a talented singer should also use her brains. Should Valen know about this?"

"I don't know who sent me a package, Eric!" Angel recalled the last time she had witnessed Jack's body, so lifeless, bloody and cold. "*Rock-n-Country Magazine* must have sent their contract negotiations for the cover shoot."

"No, I checked. The address belongs to a Haze Ranch. It's the same address where World Wide sent the limousine to pick you up where apparently you were on some secret rendezvous."

"I wasn't on a rendezvous with any man! I was stranded after my car accident!"

"Oh, that's right." He didn't believe her.

"Maybe, Mrs. Haze sent me something from Madison that I left on her ranch."

"Perhaps, but how did she get this address?"

"I didn't give out your address! I swear to you, I don't know how she acquired it!"

"Then why would she send it here, to the only office Valen doesn't have access to? Why didn't she send the package to your home?"

"I don't know. You've got to believe me. I don't know." Angel clutched the phone with her long pink nails digging into her palm.

"Valen wouldn't approve of this."

"It's not even from a man." Angel hoped it wasn't. "I know how Valen gets. I know he couldn't handle that after what his mother did to his father. I wouldn't put him through any unnecessary pain, I swear; please don't even think about telling Valen that package came for me."

"I haven't." Eric Brannett was diehard loyal to Valen but was also as protective. "But I do suggest you get down here right away and pick up this package before Valen arrives in the morning. I don't want him walking in and finding this somewhere on my desk."

Angel jumped out of bed and hurried to her dresser to find a dress. "I'll be right there! There's no reason to threaten me."

"Valen isn't the only one capable of many things."

"Believe me, I remember and know that."

＊ ＊ ＊ ＊

The letter read:

Dear Angel:

I wish I would have been able to say goodbye. I'm sorry now that I had been too tired to visit with you further. You're a very special, young woman and I enjoyed our talks together very much.

Jono told me about what happened, the car accident and how you two met. I told him, it must have been fate that brought you to our home, fate and luck from the good Lord.

Anyway, we've been keeping very busy. Jono has been repairing fences and counting cattle with the boys. I've been busy, too, sewing and baking goodies for the Pastor's bake sale.

I'm sending you some money for your car damages. I hope you don't mind.

Well, I must be going. Jono will be home soon and I need to finish cleaning up before dinner.

Please stop by the next time you're in Madison. We both miss you,

Grace Haze

"Why didn't Jono tell his grandmother I didn't want anything for the damages, that it wasn't even my car but a rental? Now look what she's done!" Angel ripped open the mailed box and a bundle of cash spilled onto the floor. Immediately, she bent over and snatched the bills before Eric Brannett returned to his office.

"I can't accept this!" She couldn't believe the amount of money Mrs. Haze had sent her as she stuffed the bills inside her large purse. "Three thousand dollars for repairs, how can they afford that? Why didn't she send a check so I could just rip it up?"

If anyone should be paying, it should be me for their hospitality and lossof livestock, Angel thought, as she seated herself slowly in Eric Brannett's chair behind his long glass-topped desk.

Angel reached for the letter and began tearing it into small pieces as she fought back her tears. "Why do you have to be so sweet, Mrs. Haze? Why do you have to care about me?" She threw the rest of the torn letter into the trash bin next to the desk. "Now I feel obligated to return this money in person."

She reached down into the box and found a wrapped package of tin foil at the bottom. Quickly, she pulled out the tin foil and peeled away one edge to discover what secrets were inside.

Chocolate chip cookies, at least a dozen of them, were packed tightly in the tin foil, and smelled absolutely delicious and homemade fresh.

She lifted one up and held it to the desk light. The cookies were large, round, soft and thick with rich, dark chocolate chips. Chocolate chip were her own mother's favorites, too; the ones she loved to bake the most.

With a long dragged out sigh, Angel blinked away the tears that had suddenly come to her eyes. "I miss you, too, Mrs. Haze," she whispered. "I wish I was with you right now on your ranch."

She lowered the tin foil container of cookies onto her lap and began tearing up the box, destroying the last of the evidence that a package had arrived for her. "Maybe, I'll see you both soon if it's possible."

Angel tossed the last of the box into the trash and leaned back into the chair. She closed her eyes and tried to forget, the people she had met in Madison so long ago. She thought she would never be able to stay their friend.

"What are you eating?" Valen entered the room from the shadows, making her wonder how long he had been inside.

Angel jerked to attention, caught in the act of doing an immeasurable sin and worrying about the extent of time Valen had been ease dropping. "A cookie."

"You do look like someone who got into the cookie jar."

"I'm sorry. I'm just surprised to see you here this time at night, that's all."

"I see." She watched him cross the room.

"Did Eric leave you that cookie?" Valen's left temple began to tick and Angel knew that no matter what she answered Valen would be argumentative.

"No, Mrs. Haze, the woman I met in Madison, Colorado sent them to me."

"You're not supposed to give out your agent's address without express permission." His brown eyes were piercing through her skin like daggers.

"I know."

"Then why did you?"

Angel pushed the cookie package on her lap to the side of the chair and then stood, readying herself. "I didn't give out the address. I merely mentioned to the woman that I'm a professional singer. I'm not sure how she was able to acquire it."

"I'll find out." Valen seated himself in a leather chair in front of the large glass plate windows that overlooked the city.

"Go ahead, I have nothing to hide."

"Really?" Valen's second finger on his left hand began tapping on the edge of the chair to a loud rhythm. "Do you like the woman in Madison?"

"Yes."

"Did she send you a letter as well?"

"Why?"

"Let me read it."

"I threw the note away. I'm terribly sorry. The letter is somewhere on the fourth floor in a waste basket. I believe it is in either Cliff's or Masterson's trash can. Would you like me to search for it?" Angel prayed her willingness to find the letter would give Valen enough peace of mind to ease his worries.

"That won't be necessary, Principessa, I can see that now."

"She said nothing of importance, anyway, or I would have remembered to keep the letter." Though his tone wasn't as sharp, his finger was continuing to tap now in a faster rhythm.

"Good, now give me what you are hiding in Brannett's chair, that silver package."

"What silver package?"

"Don't even pretend to not know. Bring me the silver package, now!"

Instantly, she ducked for the cookies and brought the container to his side. "Here you go."

He saw what was inside by a crack in the tinfoil. "Just cookies?" He ripped the package open and the cookies spilled into his lap.

"Yes, Valen." Angel's heart was pounding. Her breath was coming in short sharp pains.

Valen raised a cookie to his mouth and chewed. The pleasure of the taste showed on his face. "These are homemade?" He finished the cookie off with two more bites then went for another.

"Do you like them?"

He didn't answer. "Did you hear *Rock-N-Country Magazine* has rescheduled? I hear they are trying to get that famous rodeo cowboy again to be on the cover with you and your band."

"I suppose you'll be coming to Colorado with me?" Angel asked.

"Are you going to be visiting this new friend, Mrs. Haze, in Madison, or can I trust you to go straight to the photo shoot and then return immediately after to the airport?"

Angel knew what she must answer. "I'm only going to the *Rock-N-Country* photo shoot as scheduled."

"Good, then there is no need for me to come. I have urgent business in Italy. I'll be gone for the amount of time you will be," Valen informed after he had finished his third cookie. "Don't worry, though, I'll be calling often to keep a close eye on you. I want to make sure this trip goes as planned, not like the last time."

"I'll be fine."

"Stay away from bulls." Valen rewrapped the package and gazed into her eyes. "I want you to have a safe trip." Angel reached down to take her package from him now that he had finished eating.

"You should leave a cookie for Brannett. He loves chocolate chip."

"It was sweet of her to think of me, wasn't it?"

Valen suddenly snatched her before she could pivot back toward the desk. "What do you care if that woman is sweet?" His hands gripped her tiny frame hard against his body.

"You're hurting me."

Valen released her. His eyes were gawking at the hands that had been squeezing her arms. "I'm sorry, Angel. I was thinking of what my mother did."

"I know." She gasped. "Everything is fine, don't worry. It was nothing."

"I have to go pick up my prescription. I'll call you later."

Angel watched him leave the office, wishing she could make him understand that all those medicines he was taking to sleep were only making his problems much worse.

"Are you the 'Cowboy'?"

CHAPTER 8

A man on horseback was yards away from him, on Haze property. Jono had Wildshot by the reins and was about to tighten his saddle when he heard the rider approaching from the east.

"Well, no mind. I know who ya'r are. Ya'r the famous Cowboy."

Jono cocked a brow, gave him a sidelong glance then returned to securing Wildshot's saddle. The man was small, clean accent too strong and fake; he wasn't from around there. That didn't surprise Jono. Jono had seen too many of them—men attempting to be ranchers. Some made it; most didn't. Normally, Jono wouldn't take notice of him, if it wasn't for the gun sitting high on the stranger's hide belt.

"My name's S-Skeeter."

He's nervous, Jono noted, not a good sign. "Tell me what you want and then get off my land."

"Well, I don't know if ya' know my boy, Austin?" No response. "Well, we bought the Jenkins' ranch just east of Whiskey Creek, last week. Ya' ever hear of us?"

No response.

"All right, I'll come out with the truth. I'm from Maine." His accent dropped. "My family bought this ranch so I could research the novel I'm writing. I thought it would be easy handling a ranch. I was doing okay, at least, until this morning when I was trying to teach my son how to ride a horse."

"I didn't know the Jenkins had a well dug north of the house; it's real deep and my son was riding and fell."

Jono glanced up and the man froze. He knew exactly the well, too deep and too dry. It had been boarded up years ago because of the many Herefords that had fallen into it and broken their backs.

"My son needs your help. I wasn't sure you would help me if I wasn't a local. Skeeter is just my pen name. My boy's alive. I hear his yells. We've got a few local firefighters out there, as many as I could possibly find, but my son is pretty heavy. To be honest, he's a great son, but he shouldn't have probably been on the horse in the first place. The men told me how you wrestled a mountain lion with your bare hands, lifted a cow over a fence when it was caught, and how you saved the Tupont family. Well, if you can lift a seven hundred pound cow over a fence, you could lift my boy."

Jono mounted Wildshot's back. "Are you going to keep talking or are we going to save your boy?"

* * * *

They arrived within the hour. A small crowd of women and four men were pulling on a rope that dangled over and into the giant well with no apparent prevail.

Jono assumed it was attached to the boy somewhere. They heard the agonized whine, the cry of the boy, and it ripped at his heart.

He wasn't old, maybe thirteen. His voice was jumping up and down as he was screaming for help.

Jono dismounted and moved over to the edge of the enormous well. The well was too dark to make heads or tails of anything. The wood that once barricaded the hole was hanging over the edge by a single board. The board was the only thing left to cover this enormous opening and it was full of large spike-sized nails. If the board broke the spikes would fall and kill the boy below.

"What about the horse?" Jono asked Skeeter.

"My son says she's dead, broken back and bled to death from the fall."

"Where's the rope attached?"

"We don't need him!" a drunken voice cried out from the talk in the crowd. "Those men got it covered."

"Oh, really?" Skeeter bolted around, shaking his head in disagreement. "Why is my son still down there?" Then Skeeter pivoted to Jono and politely answered, saying, "The rope is attached around his middle."

"That's the problem. Tell him to wrap the rope around his arms and back like an X. I don't want to break the boy's ribs."

"Please," laughed the stranger, "you really believe he's got special powers?"

Jono took a deep breath and leaned into Skeeter. "You tell your boy that, or I'll break his ribs not intending to."

"Sure thing." And Skeeter yelled the command over the side of the well. Jono felt a hand pound on his back. "Hey, Cowfreak, look at me."

Turn the other cheek, Jono reminded himself as he circled toward the stranger. The man was short, too full of himself, and his breath stunk of liquor.

"You better start praying for those mighty powers."

Skeeter bravely cut in between the two men. "My son is down there and he's going to die if someone doesn't help pull him out. Now save this macho nonsense for later. The 'Cowboy' needs to help my son now."

"That's fine by me," Jono muttered; he turned to look down into the well.

Instantly, the drunken man shoved Skeeter out of the way and tightened his hand into a fist. He wanted to blindside Jono with a punch to the ribs, but another man, dressed in a firefighter's uniform, rushed out from the crowd of onlookers and seized the hand before it could strike.

"I wouldn't try to upset him if I were you. He's a legend in these parts; all El Paso County knows of the Madison 'Cowboy.'"

"Knows shit."

The firefighter held his grip. "He's wrestled bulls, mountain lions, and knocked out a poacher weighing near two-fifty; I've seen it with my own eyes! You honestly think if he decides to teach you a lesson, you'll survive more than one blow? You're wrong, Mister; you're wrong. I kindly suggest you leave your insults for someone who isn't so dangerous."

Jono was unimpressed with both of them and pivoted again to lean over the edge. The boy's cries were echoing in the chamber. Jono had had enough.

"Ready?" Jono called down to the teenager.

He heard a meek cry, "Yes, Sir."

Suddenly, Jono grabbed the rope, wrapping it tightly around both of his large palms. He dug his snakeskin cowboy boots into the dirt and pulled.

Pains began to burn in his wrist muscles, extending down the lengths of his bulging arms to his pectorals. The boy was heavy, damn heavy. But Jono only pulled harder, grabbing more rope, trusting he could not fail.

His shirt was ripping. All eyes were on him. He felt the glares piercing his back as his shirt fell to the ground. Every muscle in his enormous body was straining, aching as if they would tear and break. Jono only pulled the large boy higher.

"You need help?" he heard someone ask, but it was muffled by the gasps of disbelief.

No one was coming to his aid. Jono cursed his so-called reputation with a spit to the dirt and took another foot of rope with two giant steps back.

The rope was digging into Jono's hands, ripping his flesh more with every inch he brought the boy higher. Sweat was dripping into his eyes. His muscles were about to give, shaking involuntarily, especially his left Achilles tendon, which was levering most of the weight.

Three more feet, he lifted the boy higher. Then he didn't feel the pain anymore, didn't feel anything. Numb, his hands were going numb! His heart began to pound, afraid, afraid for the boy who might die because of his reputation of saving lives. Couldn't anyone see he needed help?

Jono glanced over his shoulder and was about to ask the firefighter for assistance, when Skeeter stepped over to the edge and extended a hand. Skeeter pulled his three-hundred-pound teenage son up over the edge.

Jono's body fell back to the ground with the snapped release of tension. At the same time, the panting young man plopped down next to Jono with his mangled broken leg extended.

He needs a doctor, Jono thought as he sat up. So did Jono, if he let himself think about how badly his hands hurt.

He felt a tap on his back and smelled the breath of the drunk again next to his ear. "I wouldn't believe it, if I didn't see it with my own eyes. It's all true! It's all true!" Jono ignored him, watching the teenager wipe away his tears and his father embrace him. Jono nodded to the boy who was smiling at him.

"Thank you, 'Cowboy,'" said the boy.

Just as he spoke, the boards that once covered the well fell into the depths of the darkness and everyone heard the loud thundering crash.

Skeeter reached out and grasped Jono's bloody hand and shook it hard. "Thank you, 'Cowboy,' I'll be taking him to the closest doctor's office now."

The teenager's face lit up, dimples appearing. "The 'Cowboy' saved me!"

"Yes." Skeeter patted his son's back. "The legend himself."

"A legend; am I?" with that, Jono Haze stood and strolled back to Wildshot. He was in need of a bath, a long hot bath to forget his aches and pains. He also wanted to clear his head; he never had doubted his strength before.

Wildshot nickered as Jono approached and maneuvered himself into the saddle. Then with a nod to the crowd, they were off, the legend and his horse. Jono's short blondish-brown hair was blowing in the wind. His golden necklace was pounding against his chest as the massive animal raced proud and firm between his legs.

Yells were flying through the air from the locals hollering from behind. There were cries of gratitude, calls of thanks to the man they all called their legendary hero.

CHAPTER 9

In front of the camera, Angel liked to play the seductress. She felt alive and free.

"Perfect, Angel, sway your hair." She flipped her raven curls and made love to the camera with bedroom eyes, her luscious body curves.

"Hold it. Hold it. Now, begin singing."

For her latest music video, Angel was modeling a $180,000 dollar Lancobi dress of woven gold silk and bead-covered crystals. Styled after the Cleopatra era, the shimmering masterpiece and head gear was constructed to beguile and tantalize. Her stomach was exposed. Gold and black scarves dangled from her skinny arms to form a glamorous cape and crown.

"Work it, Girl," the director crowed.

Angel leaned her hip against a golden backdrop and gave an off-the-shoulder glance while she sang. This sexy pose was her calling card. This was her unforgettable smile which had garnered her millions of fans.

Her long raven hair was flowing down her back to her tiny waist in large girlish curls. Her gray eyes lined black like a tiger's were shocking in contrast to her alabaster skin.

Angel felt beautiful.

"Yes, that's it," the director praised. "Turn around and lean over a bit." Angel followed his instructions.

"Now, bend maybe a little more." He licked his lips. "Even more."

"Like hell she's bending over more!" Valen's furious scream could be heard across the entire studio as he thundered onto the set to confront the director.

Valen gave him a cold stare. "Your bending over gives everyone more of a silhouette of your breasts!" Valen told her. "The lights shine through your dress!"

A hundred knives couldn't have cut through the tension in the room, or the anger in Valen's eyes toward the director. With hands locked into fists, Valen was ready to kill.

The Video Director stood up from his chair, cowering back at the sight of the man notorious for having a terrible temperament.

"Your name is Roy Valear, right?"

"Yes," the director gulped.

"I see you anywhere near Angel again, I will stick your cameras where you will never find them, understood?"

"Understood." The director tried to exit, but Valen, in three massive strides, snatched him by the arm.

"Who hired you, Eric Brannett or Jamie Dennis?"

"Eric Brannett."

"Tell Mr. Brannett that there was a problem today. If Eric has any questions why I am permanently removing her from this set, tell him to call me."

"Yes, I'll tell him." Valen released the director's arm and immediately he and his crew ran for the door to escape.

"The nerve of that imbecile! Did you know what he was staring at?" Valen swung a fist at a piece of the pyramid backdrop and tossed it across the studio. A shard of glass cut into his gloved hand.

"No."

Blood was seeping from his white satin glove down to the floor. "He was staring at your breasts through the dress. With the lights, you could see everything."

"I didn't know."

Valen tried to grab her but missed by a few inches. Blood spewed across the golden scarf covering her left shoulder. "Did you want him to see? How could you not know?"

"I'm so sorry."

"People will think you are a whore! You want the world to see your breasts like that?"

She watched his bloody gloved hand and suddenly stopped. "Valen, look at your hand."

Valen's eyes shot toward his hand covered in blood. "What happened?"

Angel realized he had been so angry at the director that he hadn't realized yet that he had punched a part of the set and cut his hand badly. He was bleeding profusely. "We need to get you to a hospital."

"What did I do to myself?"

She realized that his temper was dissipating caused by the shock of finding his hand injured. "You got angry and broke off a piece of the glass scenery. I'll call your doctor."

"No," he ordered. "It's just a cut. You can mend it. I don't want the press to learn of this."

"You need to think of yourself first." Valen suddenly smiled.

"I'll be fine."

Valen leaned down and placed a gentle kiss on her cheek. A single strand of her black hair fell onto her cheek next to his lips and he brushed the unruly hair away underneath her golden head piece. "Okay, you call the doctor and bring me my pills. They are in the back of the car."

"You don't need any more pills, Valen."

"They will work for the pain." His lips were hovering above hers, inching downwards.

"Why don't you ever listen to me?"

"Because I'd rather shut you up." He pressed his lips down swiftly to hers, capturing and claiming what he deemed to be his.

Angel was his.

His tongue plunged into her mouth. Angel became instantly intoxicated. It was rare for Valen to show affection. She arched her feminine frame against his; rubbing, relishing every moment she knew would not last. Her nails began clawing into his suit jacket, trying to persuade him to continue.

He broke away.

She immediately reached for him, pulling him once more into her arms. Her eyes were begging. Her breath was sweet and hot against his lips. "I want you to show me how much you love me. I'll be your medicine."

Valen pulled away. "I don't like when you talk like that."

She saw right through his angry façade. His left temple wasn't ticking. "I'm far from a tramp and you know it. I've been saving myself for when we will finally get married, Valen."

Valen ignored the implied question and changed the subject. "There are things which we must discuss about your schedule. I've changed Eric's plans for you."

"I'm not going to Colorado later this week?"

"Yes, but now. There is a limousine waiting for you outside to take you to my jet. You will be spending the night with your friends Billy and Daisy, not in a hotel room with no protection."

"But I thought I wasn't to leave until the red-eye."

"It would be in the best interests of Worldwide if you arrived early instead of late like other rock stars so often do."

"So, I am to stay with Daisy?"

"Yes, Daisy and her husband."

"Daisy?"

"I thought that would please you."

"I haven't seen her in years, since she quit playing drums for Twisted Youth."

"She and her husband moved to Pinon last year. It is not that far from Madison," Valen said. "Jesu, another employee of mine, will drive you from their house to *Rock-N-Country* in the morning."

"Whatever you wish," she said.

He moved her toward the door, leading in a slow casual pace so she could keep up in her five-inch-high heels. "If every wish came true, Principessa, you would be traveling with me to Italy, not Colorado."

His words halted her step. "Valen, you're acting as if you don't want me to do the cover of *Rock-N-Country*."

The sunlight streaming through the glass door nearly blinded her as it reflected off her dress. She squinted as he leaned down and gave her one last kiss. "Go ahead and go back home. I'll see you when I return from Italy."

As he hurried out onto the street, Angel yelled, "Go to the hospital to take care of that hand!"

CHAPTER 10

Angel wondered if she could trust the driver. "Then you'll keep your mouth shut?"

"For ten thousand dollars, I'll keep quiet." Jesu placed his hand on top of his heart. "If I tell Valen, may I be struck down."

* * * *

Freedom, peace and serenity came over Angel in waves of emotion. She felt at ease. The air was fresh and clean. On top of the hill, far in the distance, large cattle roamed across the grasslands beneath the blue, cloudless sky.

The Haze ranch felt like home, ageless, timeless, and oblivious to the modern world. There was such natural beauty in the land and house before her as the limousine rolled to a stop at the side of the sunflower garden.

Mrs. Haze was in her wheelchair, knitting on the front porch, as Angel exited the limousine before her driver had enough time to assist.

"Hello, Mrs. Haze!" she called. Mrs. Haze held out her arms from her wheelchair and Angel embraced her.

"Hello, Deary! I'm so glad you've come to visit."

"I couldn't resist."

"I suppose you received the money I sent for repairs to the car."

"Yes, that is why I had to come. I'm returning your money. Didn't Jono tell you that I didn't need any money for the damages?"

"He didn't. To be honest, I sent the money selfishly."

"Selfishly?"

"He's been moping around here since you left. I knew I had to bring you back somehow," Mrs. Haze said. There was silence for a few minutes as Angel realized Jono had missed her, too.

"Sit a spell, Deary. Let's talk a while."

Angel sashayed past her and lowered herself into the rocking chair. Then she crossed her legs and rested her head against the chair's white wooden back, relaxing from her journey. "It's such a beautiful day. Don't you agree?"

"Yes, it is. Colorado's lovely this time of year."

"Have you always lived in Colorado?" Angel removed the money from her dress' side pocket and placed it on the table between them. "If you don't mind my asking."

Mrs. Haze lowered her quilt. "I was born in Georgia. When I was seventeen, my father decided to take us to Madison to meet a friend of his who was Native American. That's where I met my husband and fell in love."

"Was owning cattle ranch your husband's idea?"

"Oh no, it was mine. He sure took a liking to it. I just wish my husband could have seen this ranch grow like this before he died." Mrs. Haze looked out over the property. "I believe he would have been very proud of his son, especially because Jono built the house from the ground up."

"Jono built all this?"

"Yes, to make my dreams of living in a big house come true."

"How wonderful!"

"Jono started when he was a teenager and finished construction by his eighteenth birthday. I still don't quite believe it. A boy that young with such talent for building and taking care of things." Mrs. Haze shifted in her wheelchair. "He's very different, my grandson, in a great way."

Angel's heart skipped a beat. "I've never met anyone quite like him."

"He likes you, too, you know."

"Pardon?"

"Not too many people have raised their voice to him. He said he started falling for you the moment you raised your voice and yelled at him on the horse ride."

Angel blushed. "He told you about that?"

"Just what I need to know," Mrs. Haze said. "The rest, I don't."

Angel heard the pound of hooves. In the distance, a horse and rider were approaching like the wind. Fast and powerful, Wildshot raced across the grasslands as if he were trying to beat time itself. The man on top of the stallion, Angel would recognize anywhere. Jono Haze was coming.

"Something's wrong!" Mrs. Haze tossed her quilt onto the table and began quickly wheeling herself to the porch door.

Jono pulled in the reins and Wildshot halted in his tracks by the side of the vegetable garden. Immediately, he leaped out of the saddle and ran to his grandmother's chair. "Where's the ax?"

"You left it on the kitchen table this morning."

Without hesitation, he rushed past his grandmother and disappeared into the house. His cowboy boots were making loud thunderous crashes against the wooden floor until he was again by his grandmother's side, carrying what he had been seeking.

"What's wrong, Son?"

"An accident at the Lanson property, the barn collapsed while the horses were inside!" Then as quick as Jono came, he was gone, riding like lightning on the back of his mighty stallion.

It was as if Jono hadn't even seen her. "Follow him, Deary."

"I've never seen a man move so fast. I've seen a horse run like that."

"Follow him!" Angel redirected her attention from the distancing horse and rider as soon as she heard the panic in Mrs. Haze's voice.

"Follow him! Help if you can."

Angel Frederick did not have to be asked again.

CHAPTER 11

The rain was beating hard against the windowpanes as a woman entered his office in Italy.

"Buonasera, Valentino. Buonasera."

Valen glanced up from his paperwork. His bandaged hand was bleeding again. "Chiami un medico, per favore."

The woman ran from his office just as his phone began to ring. He smiled. "Pronto, Principessa."

"I am going to be a little late for my photo shoot. Please, don't be angry. I'm fine, just slept in."

"All right." He breathed. "Thank you for calling. If I had heard you were late, I would have worried."

"Don't, I'm fine. I'm not that far from *Rock-N-Country* photo shoot now. I won't be long."

"I'll call them and explain your tardiness. We'll talk later."

"How is your hand? What did your doctor say?"

He saw the blood seeping through the bandages. "It's going to need stitches, but I'm fine."

"I'll call you after the photo shoot," Angel said.

Valen hung up the phone slowly as the vein in his left temple began to tick.

* * * *

Angel watched as Jono broke through about half a dozen boards to free a group of horses from a pile of rubble that at one time had been a barn.

Jesu was dripping with perspiration; his sandy blond hair was frazzled and dirty. Quickly, he interrupted Angel ogling over the "Cowboy". "We better go, Miss Frederick. The horses were pulled out. You're late for *Rock-N-Country*."

"Just one more minute until I can talk to Jono."

"We better leave. I'll wait behind the wheel."

Jono crossed his cowboy boots as he leaned his large frame against the limousine. "Sounds like you have to go, Angel."

"Where did your horse go?" she questioned while a hot shiver raced through her body.

"He ran off with the Larson's horses to play."

"Are you ever serious? Your horse just left you stranded."

"All I've got to do is whistle; Wildshot will be back." Jono's sweat intoxicated the air. His scent didn't make her want to leave the vicinity. This time, in fact, she didn't want to part from him and took several steps across the golden grass to get closer. "I can give you a ride if need be."

He changed the subject. "It's good to see you again. But you've got a place you're supposed to be at," he reminded. "Why don't you come back to the ranch when you are done?"

"I learned that *Rock-N-Country* is already going to be a disaster. The famous 'Cowboy' isn't going to teach me how to ride a horse, so it'll probably take me most of the day to get the shot that the photographer had originally wanted," Angel said.

"That's a shame." Jono's body glistened with every word as he inhaled and exhaled. "Would you like to come back to Madison, next Friday, for my grandmother's birthday party?"

"It's your grandmother's birthday?"

His golden earring shimmered when he leaned over to wipe the dirt off one of his skin boots. "I know she had been planning on asking you herself."

"She didn't mention it."

"You've already seen her today?"

"Yes, I was there when you ran in and grabbed the ax. You were running so fast, you didn't see me."

"I'm sorry." His big blue eyes danced apologetically. "I was worried that the horses would be crushed. I would have at least said hello had I not been so focused."

"That's how I was able to find you here." Angel wanted to kiss him but thought of Valen. "That sure was something, you saving all those horses. I would have been here sooner, had my limousine not taken so long."

"Limousines aren't really made for bogging in the mud." He smiled. "They are made more for carrying pretty ladies like yourself."

She blushed, glancing back at the limousine which was now covered by dirt. "I am just glad that you were able to save those horses."

"Our town vet was called in, but from what I've seen they look pretty good."

Her eyes met his. His deep blue eyes were twinkling down into hers. He was bewitching. "Thank goodness, you are a hero."

He slowly lifted one of her hands to his bare chest. He began to lean in for a kiss when suddenly his hand went over the giant diamond on her fourth finger. Shock and then disappointment showed in his eyes. "Why didn't you tell me?"

Suddenly, Jono turned and whistled for Wildshot. "Wait!"

The powerful horse was instantly racing from the southern grasslands. It was like someone had lit a fire under the horse's hooves.

"I should have told you that I got engaged," Angel said.

He mounted his horse and said, "Love is patient; love is kind. Love is not jealous, it does not put on airs, it is not snobbish. Love is never rude, it is not self-seeking, it is not prone to anger, neither does it brood over injuries. Love does not rejoice in what is wrong but rejoices in the truth. There is no limit to love's forbearance, to its trust, its hope, its power to endure."

"That was beautiful."

A hawk cried in the background as it was circling lower in the sky toward the west. The sun peeked out behind the clouds as the grass swayed in the wind. In all, there was peace. Angel knew in this land, in this man, lived a happiness she would never be able to understand.

"It's my favorite Bible verse."

She was speechless, taken aback by a man so unselfish and forgiving. He was so unlike any other man she had ever met.

His eyes never wavered from hers. "I will be patient, Angel. I know how I feel about you."

He was about to snap the reins, but Angel moved to his side, looking upward at him with tear-filled eyes. "I have feelings for you, too, Jono. Just, please, don't wait for something that can never be. We come from two different worlds. We can't ever be anything more than friends."

"Are we so different?" he asked.

She lifted her hand and placed it gently on his leg. "I'll do my best to come next Friday for your grandmother's birthday. I like her very much and would love to come celebrate."

"I'll be looking forward to seeing my friend then." He leaned down and kissed her on her cheek.

A hot shiver ran down her spine and through every inch of her body. She took a deep breath and stepped away. "You, too."

Before she could say goodbye, he was gone—the only man Angel knew she could honestly fall in love with.

One week later…

CHAPTER 12

She didn't blatantly lie, Angel told herself. It was only a minor misstatement of the whole truth. She was in fact visiting her friend Daisy in Colorado to deliver a baby gift. And she was going to stay in a fine hotel tonight. However, the hotel would be in Madison instead of Pinon where Daisy lived and where Valen assumed—okay, it was a lie.

She felt guilty, of course she did. Angel cared for Valen deeply. But overall, she knew there was no other way to break free and visit Mrs. Haze on her birthday if she hadn't lied about where she was going.

Daisy lowered her body, nine months pregnant, carefully onto her Victorian sofa across from Angel. "I'm so glad you decided to fly in and deliver our baby gift in person, Angel." Daisy was a beautiful brunette woman, with striking features and long, silky legs. Her high cheek-boned face was beaming. To Angel's recollection, she had never seen her ex-business associate so jubilant. "I hope Valen didn't mind."

"No, not at all," Angel remembered his brooding expression and avoided Daisy's eyes.

"Are you sure? Valen is known for keeping a close eye on you."

"I'm glad I've come." Angel handed Daisy a gift box wrapped in yellow paper. "I've missing working with you and Bill."

A motorcycle roar reverberated throughout the house. "Speaking of Billy, he's home!" Angel turned her head toward the door as Billy strolled into his Colorado home, carrying a motorcycle helmet. Six foot two, and as handsome as a Ken doll, Bill was one of the highest paid male models in the fashion industry. He was handsome, blond and sexy, from his slicked back long hair to his perfectly tight black jeans. From beer commercials to main character rolls on the silver screen, Bill was multi-talented, and a man no one seemed to be able to forget, especially Daisy.

Bill Marcami plopped down on the sofa next to his wife and flipped on a football game on the television set with the remote control. "If it isn't Angel." He smiled at Angel then kissed his wife hello. "Doesn't my wife look gorgeous?"

"Yes, Bill," Angel agreed. "I was just about to ask her if it's a boy or a girl."

Bill smirked, showing off his pearly teeth. "It's a boy!"

Daisy elbowed him lovingly in the ribs. "He wants to be the father of a N.F.L. star."

He laughed, patted her belly and smacked it with a kiss. "And he's gonna buy Daddy season tickets every Christmas."

Daisy rolled her eyes. "Such a ham, what if he wants to take ballet?"

Bill tossed his motorcycle helmet to the floor and began removing his leather jacket. "Then I'll buy him tights and go to his performances."

Angel was impressed. "There's a softer side to you, after all, Bill!"

"Like hell." With one eye, Bill stared at the television set; with the other, he glanced down to the newspaper that was laying on the sofa beside him.

"Oh," Daisy elbowed him, "that 'Cowboy' made headlines again."

"Again?" He unfolded the newspaper. "What page?"

"Page 3, C."

"So how have you been feeling, Daisy?" Angel interrupted. "You told me you were having some difficulties."

"Oh, I'm much better than the last time we talked. Now I just can't control my bladder any better than the swelling."

"Yesterday," Bill cut into the conversation as he turned a page of the newspaper, "we went to the next door neighbor's house. Daisy sat on this blush velvet couch. And all of a sudden, she got this look on her face like… Ouch!" He stopped speaking the moment she gave him a sharp jab to the ribs and the evil eye. "I take it that story's out."

"Out!" Leaning back with a large masculine grin, Bill decided to read the article on the Cowboy.

"Did you know my husband wants to name our child after a football player?"

Bill rose, went to the kitchen and returned with a beer. "I don't see anything wrong with that."

"I see." Angel raised her hand to her mouth, trying to hide her amusement. "Well, you both seem ecstatic about the baby even if you don't agree on the name."

Bill returned to his seat, shaking his head as he began reading the newspaper article again.

"So, when is your wedding to Valen?" Daisy asked. "I had heard that he proposed. Have you two decided on a wedding date yet?" Angel noticed how Bill was consumed in the newspaper, even missing the last touchdown made by the Broncos on the television set.

"We might have the wedding in the spring of next year. That will give me plenty of time to plan."

Bill gasped. "That cowboy's a hero again."

Daisy leaned in, placed her head on his shoulder. "I thought you would find this article interesting."

"Interesting, I can hardly believe this guy doesn't join a football team!" "One of these days, Angel, some writer is going to get a hold of this 'Cowboy's' life story and make it into a best seller."

Daisy glanced up at her husband. "It's hard to believe that any human being can be that invincible."

"That's because you don't watch football." Bill smirked.

"What if he's not human?" Angel laughed.

"Could you imagine what kind of person he is, knowing he has all this power and strength?" Bill said.

"What if he's a total jerk?"

"I never thought about it, that way," Daisy said.

Bill rested the paper on his lap. "You know, you're right, Honey. If the 'Cowboy' wrestled one of my favorite football players, I wouldn't want to bet on who would win." Bill paused. "I'm surprised the Paparazzi isn't following this guy around."

"People are afraid of him."

"The press isn't afraid of anyone."

"The 'Cowboy' is a freak of nature, Darling. Even all those rag magazines would call him a hoax."

"Well, I better be going," Angel announced, rising from her seat. "I'm getting very tired."

"Oh, please stay awhile. I'm sorry. This man is just so unbelievable. He's already saved so many lives; people can't even count them anymore. He once… never mind." Daisy smiled as Angel yawned. "I can see you're very tired.

Angel yawned again. "Well, I'll be back sometime tomorrow after I rest up. Jet lag, you know how it is. I'll just call Valen before I go and tell him I'm going to sleep."

"Weren't you supposed to meet the 'Cowboy' for that *Rock-N-Country Magazine* photo shoot?" Bill suddenly recalled.

Angel nodded. "He couldn't do the interview or help me learn how to ride a horse. He had some sort of scheduling problem."

"Or maybe he wanted to suck cow's blood." Bill lifted his arms and laughed.

* * * *

Angel returned to Madison a week later to attend Mrs. Haze's birthday party. Valen hadn't returned to the States from Italy so there was no guilt to hold her back from going.

Angel kept telling herself that Mrs. Haze was a wonderful woman who was her new friend. She had every right to be there to celebrate

Mrs. Haze's birthday. Valen hadn't even returned to the States from Italy, so why should she even make a big deal of this next trip? Why feel so guilty? Angel contemplated on her feelings.

Angel exited the stretch limousine. The luxury car certainly stood out in Madison. Angel noticed many gawkers including one large man standing by the doorway of the gas station.

She walked toward the store's entrance. The man moved closer, lifting his cowboy hat as she approached.

"What's a rich bitch like you doing in Madison?" the stranger asked. He grabbed the store's door handle so she couldn't enter the store.

"Excuse me?" Angel shrieked.

He laughed, cruelly. "We don't need anyone who works for White feather coming here." The man was tall. His hair was long and dark brown. He appeared to be Native American with dark eyes and tan skin.

"Please get out of my way! I just want to find a hotel around here. I have no idea who Whitefeather is!"

"My name is LaFordge. You mean you don't know who I am?"

"Jesu!" Angel called frantically to her personal limousine driver. Jesu wasn't behind the wheel or pumping gas.

"His practice is tearing apart our community."

"Please, Sir," Angel felt his hand grab her arm. "I'm here visiting Grace and Jono Haze. I have no understanding of what you are talking about."

His hand suddenly released her as if it had been scorched the moment she spoke their names.

"That's right, LaFordge," spoke a deep voice. A dark shadow fell across the man's back, covering him and Angel completely. Slowly, the man pivoted, discovering Jono was beside them on top of his mighty steed.

"Do you have a problem with Angel visiting us?" Out of nowhere, Jono had come to her rescue. Angel rushed to stand beside Wildshot, never so happy to see a man in her life.

"I suggest you give this lady an apology." Jono didn't even need to dismount to make LaFordge feel like crawling underneath a rock. "Unless you want her to think my brother's as mean as a rattlesnake."

LaFordge immediately spoke to her. "I'm sorry, Miss. It seems I mistook you for the city folk who work for that Medicine Man, Whitefeather."

Jono laughed. "Are you still out to destroy him?"

"Whitefeather is bad news! If you had any sense, you'd listen to me and stay the hell away from him!"

"He is a doctor."

"A doctor who doesn't respect our culture or our ways." LaFordge spit.

Jono smiled. "Don't worry, Angel, he's really very sweet once you get to know him." LaFordge grinned and began walking away. He tipped his black cowboy hat to Angel.

"We'll talk about this after Maw's birthday party, LaFordge." Jono dismounted. He was finely dressed in a button-down white shirt and blue denim jeans. His five o'clock shadow had been shaved, causing every rugged feature to be visible.

Angel could not tear her eyes off the gorgeous Jono before her; her gaze drifted up and down him, while she attempted to catch her uneven breath.

"Are you all right, Angel?"

She stuttered. "Why was your brother so angry about my knowing this Whitefeather fellow?"

"It's a local thing," was all he answered, dismounting.

Her gaze drifted to his dark hands that were every bit as rough and calloused as the man who had grabbed her, but Jono's made her tremble, made her wish to be in his arms. "How many brothers do you have?"

"Three. Two live here in Madison. One lives up north."

"Are they all so frightening?"

Jono laughed. "Not to me, but maybe to an outsider they might be. We're actually all very close. We just give each other space and have differences over local politics."

"It looks like you saved me again!" He swallowed, hard, and then pushed an unruly black raven curl covering her cheek behind one ear.

"You're always near," she blinked against the brightness of the afternoon sun, "when I need you." Her body moved subconsciously. On her tippy toes, she swayed. Her lips met his cheek in gratitude.

This time Jono didn't resist. His lips moved for hers as a burning fire. Angel had never known such desire. She began to faint the moment his lips met hers. He sensed this and clamped his hands around her waist to support her.

Stars, glory and fire tied into heaven! The feel of him, being in her arms, overwhelmed her very senses. Angel couldn't believe kissing Jono would feel this perfect, even now. She couldn't get enough. She gasped into his mouth, and he silenced her again with his tongue, claiming her.

Angel was trembling, willing and wishing to give him affection.

Jono pulled away. "I shouldn't be doing this. You're in love with another, or at least you think you're in love with another."

"It's all right." Her lips were swollen from their meeting.

"Forgive me."

"I forgive you."

He took a deep breath and regained his self-control. "So did you come to see me or did you come for the party?"

"Your grandmother, for her..." She couldn't lie to him. "Both of you, really."

"The ranch is still quite a ways ahead."

She remembered her purpose for being at the store. "I came here to ask the clerk if there was a hotel in Madison."

"There isn't one, Angel, not in Madison." He patted Wildshot and then tightened the saddle. "You'll have to stay at the ranch. We've got plenty of room."

"You're not lying, are you? There really isn't a hotel or motel in Madison?"

They spoke the answer in unison: "I don't lie." "You don't lie."

He smiled, this time with ease. "You're in Madison. Up the road there's a church, bar, restaurant, hardware and a few seed stores. Besides, my home is your home."

Her heart skipped a beat. "Then I guess I have no choice on where I will stay."

* * * *

From the side of the building, Jesu slid a camera back into his jacket pocket. The picture he had just taken, of Angel and Jono kissing, was worth at least a million.

CHAPTER 13

Jono came forward and took Angel's hand. "I'm glad I came into town to pick up my grandmother's gift."

"So am I." The heat from his hand was making her shiver. "What did you buy her?"

He nodded and began leading her into the store, taking her by the arm. "I'll show you."

Everything from motor oil to clothes was stacked on shelves or hanging on racks. Angel glanced over the clutter until she spotted a shiny silver sewing machine perched in the side window of the store. "Let me guess, that's her present—the sewing machine and table!"

Jono winked.

"Oh, it's perfect," she said.

"I was going to pay for it and pick it up right before her party. I don't want my grandmother finding it before then. And believe me, she'll try."

"The sewing table it's sitting on is also beautiful," Angel commented, thinking on how his mother would admire its brown country design.

"For now, I'm just going to set the sewing machine up for her on the kitchen table until I build her one."

Angel burst with excitement. "Why don't I get her the table?"

"That's sweet of you to offer. But it's too much. My grandmother will get upset if you spend so much money when I can just build her one."

"Nonsense!" Angel broke away and scurried past him to converse with the convenience store clerk.

Jono glanced around the store and noticed how every patron's eyes were on them. "I'll be waiting outside."

Angel heard the store door close, the rush of air flowing past her. She realized that Jono made her feel more alive every second they were together.

The way his eyes caressed her and the way he touched her so lovingly, Angel knew that he had feelings for her, too. He made his feelings known by every action.

She wished she could have met him years ago, before meeting Valen. Shaking off her sudden uneasiness, Angel spoke to the woman behind the counter. "I'd like to purchase the sewing table. My friend will pick it up tomorrow when he comes to get the machine."

"That'll be two hundred dollars." The woman croaked the words nervously.

"All right." Angel fumbled through her purse until her hand clutched her wallet. Every person in the store was looking at her. Angel noticed that people were staring as she lifted her hand full of money. Then, something caught her eye.

Inside a glass case behind the counter, a single hat was dangling on a nail. It was old, broad-rimmed with black draped around the crown. Styled after the heroes and legends of the sacred West, it even had the tightening pull string.

In her mind's eye Angel pictured Jono, on the back of Wildshot, racing with the wind across the Colorado grasslands, wearing this very hat proudly on his head.

"I'll take that hat, too, please."

"That's not for sale! I bought it myself at the charity auction last year. It was the one the Cowboy was wearing when he saved that kid from the mountain lion! It is a collector's item."

"Well then it's perfect for the man I'm buying it for."

"Does he want it back? Is that it? Is the 'Cowboy' mad that it was auctioned off?"

Angel wondered what the woman meant.

"Please, if my gas and convenience store is ever in danger and we need his help then I want to be able to call on him. I don't want him upset." The woman's mouth dropped.

"Here, take it."

Angel handed her the money as the cowboy hat was being tossed to her across the counter. "It was nice doing business with you." Angel smiled then walked out the door, wondering what the woman had been babbling about.

Jono was shaking hands with an older gentleman next to Wildshot as Angel approached. The man moved away before she could reach their side.

"Jono," Angel called, and he looked down. "Look what I bought for you." She handed the hat to him as his blue eyes widened.

"Angel?"

"I know. It used to be worn by that famous cowboy."

Jono shook his head. "People think that this hat has special powers." He pushed the hat back down to her. "I can't wear it as long as it's got that silly superstition attached to it."

"You're kidding, right?"

Jono took a deep breath and lowered his frame to her level by bending at his knees. "Ever since that crazed mountain lion was killed, the people of Madison have thought that the 'Cowboy' and his hat have all these special powers." He shrugged. "I don't know why. It's nothing but a beat-up, old hat."

Never in her life had anyone refused a gift from her. Angel became instantly hurt, confused and outraged by Jono's lack of gratitude for something she had only done to please him. "Don't be dumb, Jono. Keep the hat! It's worth a lot of money in these parts, because of those superstitions."

"Don't call me dumb!" Jono's broad shoulders steeled themselves. "I was building up my father's ranch and stables, raising cattle instead of going to college. Even my grandmother couldn't put food on the table after she fell downstairs. So, I did the best I could. I may not have a college education, but I am far from dumb."

Before Jono could say another word to defend his intelligence, she flung her arms around his waist and hugged him tightly. She was sorry. How could she have been so insensitive? The last thing she desired was to hurt Jono's feelings. "I didn't mean it."

"You just hit my two sore spots," his arms rose and clung to her sides as if they were a part of her, "those silly superstitions and me being smart."

"You are smart. That's not what I meant to imply."

"Don't worry. No one's called me dumb since Jenny's birthday party. That's something else I should explain to you about who I am."

"I like you the way you are, Jono. Your past doesn't matter to me. You're my friend. I've never met anyone so caring or trustworthy."

"Learning from books is real important, but God gave me certain talents, too." Jono sighed deeply.

"You're a wonderful person and that means more to me than anything, Jono."

"Some people don't think so. They think college degrees mean more than talent. I bet they can't lasso a calf from fifty feet away."

She smiled. "No."

His blue eyes suddenly sparkled. "The most important thing to me is that I have people in my life who accept me for who I am as a person, and you do, more than anyone else besides my family."

She contemplated his admiration, then inquired, "You'll accept my gift then."

"I can't," he said. "I'm just a man, thanking God every day for the strength that he's given me. If it wasn't for the gifts He gave me, I wouldn't be able to do what I can to help others."

"You are as much of a hero as that 'Cowboy.' I've never met a man like you in my entire life, Jono." She touched the hat being held by one enormous hand. "Keep the hat."

"I can't, Angel."

It meant the world to her, for him to accept what she had purchased. She moved her hand to his and asked wholeheartedly, "Please."

"The hat isn't worth me losing your friendship by me having to explain more."

She snapped her hand back. "I don't understand."

"Don't be upset with me. I can't take it." She snatched the hat out of his hands then headed for the convenience store's entrance.

"Angel!" he called, and when she didn't stop, Jono took a few fast strides to be at her side. "Angel, wait!"

She faced him.

"What's really the issue here? Why are you so upset? You should be happy you'll get to use the money for a better purpose."

"I bought it because you're my friend."

"I am your friend without you buying me a thing."

"I know that Jono. That's the kind of person you are," she said. "Well, don't worry. I won't buy you another gift."

"Angel." As she tried to walk away, his hands gripped her shoulders from behind. "What's really wrong?"

"I only tried to give you something." She yanked her shoulders from out of his grasp.

He moved forward, reached around her and grasped the hat out of her clutches. "Angel, tell me. What is it?"

She halted and pivoted to glare up at him.

The hat was perched on Jono's magnificent head; his features appeared solid in the flowing sunlight. The wind was tickling his hair. In his enormous presence, she was enveloped by his aura.

He looked just as she had envisioned in the store, like a well-admired sheriff in an old western town—a man, who would fight bravely for peace and justice, even in a land where peace was nonexistent.

She lost her breath, gazing at him with the hat on. All her sadness, all her anger suddenly vanished. She wanted to tell him exactly how she felt. Angel knew she had to. "I bought the hat because you're my hero. You're everything I've ever wanted in a man."

Jono lowered his head and tightened the hat's pull string around his thick tan neck. "That's about the nicest thing anyone's ever said to me."

"It's true. It's almost like fate made me get into that car accident so I would meet you, or even find you here today," Angel whispered. "It's as if we were meant to be together somehow."

"Then from this moment on, I'll be proud to wear this hat, Angel." She smiled. "And every time I do, I'll remember the reason why you gave it to me." He tapped his hat, gentlemanly. "Because I agree, we are made to be together… somehow."

CHAPTER 14

Throughout the night, Valen watched the rain from his office windowsill as he waited for another phone call from Angel.

She had only called once earlier. He hadn't heard from her since.

Valen picked up the telephone receiver and placed the phone to his ear. "Damn!" He slammed it back down. "What's wrong with me? She's fine!"

There was a knock on the door, and Valen pivoted while closing the office window curtains.

"Caffe?" he heard his secretary inquire.

"Go away."

How could he proficiently begin this working day without knowing where Angel was staying, which hotel? Valen crossed the room and again picked up the telephone.

He willed it to ring.

"She's fine. She's got to be fine."

Ring! Ring!

"Do you know where Angel's staying?" Valen's voice asked over the phone to Eric Brannett.

"No, I don't. You do realize that it's the middle of the night in the States. Can't this wait until morning?"

"I think something is terribly wrong, Eric. I've hardly heard from Angel. I called Bill's and he and Daisy haven't heard from her or even know what hotel she's staying at."

"What did she tell you last time you two talked?"

"I don't know. All she said is she was going to bed, but that was many hours ago. She hasn't called me since."

"Calm down. She was on a plane for hours to get to Colorado. She probably fell asleep right after she checked in."

"I should have never fired her guards!"

"You know the reason as well as I." Eric Brannett rolled over onto his side in bed, clutching the phone. "Jack."

Valen slid into his office chair and looked over his desk that was cluttered with Pinon hotel numbers. "Jack." He breathed the name not in victory, but in sorrow.

"I shouldn't have said that name." Eric Brannett gulped.

"It is because of his murder that I fired the guards. She needed me to begin trusting her. Firing her guards changed her whole attitude. And soon she will be my wife, and that is more important."

"Angel would never be unfaithful again."

"No, she would never fall prey to another man. No, she loves me now. Jack was a mistake she made when she was young. Trusting her, now, is all that's kept me sane since I fired those guards."

Eric Brannett yawned. "She's just asleep, my friend. I would know if anything was wrong. I hired the limousine company in Colorado, remember?"

Valen cocked a smug grin. "Yes, we never did commit to not hiring her drivers, now did we?" Eric Brannett laughed. An arm wrapped around him, a long, silky feminine arm.

Valen rubbed his aching head. "I woke you, my apologies. I was just worried about her. Her whole Colorado trip has caused me nothing but anxiety."

"It's only natural for you to worry," Eric Brannett consoled. "It's instinct for every man to worry about his mate, to want to protect them, especially in the kind of world we live in today."

"She's alone traveling abroad." Valen scowled.

"Don't get on America, my friend, or we'll argue until morning. America has made us rich as kings."

Valen smiled "That reminds me; you haven't spent much time on my yacht."

"You have a fleet of them." Eric Brannett felt the woman's hand rubbing his stomach. "I'll settle for the four of us on a long, well-deserved cruise vacation."

"Done," Valen finalized. "And I'll even salute to the Statute of Liberty with an apology."

Eric Brannett was more than distracted by the woman in his bed. "You'll do just that."

"I'm sorry, Eric. How early is it in New York?" Valen clicked open his golden pocket watch out of his tailored vest and sighed.

"Too early for you to be concerned about Angel; she's probably still asleep."

Over the phone Valen overheard Eric's girlfriend moaning for him to hang up and please her. Valen closed his watch, disgusted with himself. "Well, I'll let you get back to your duties, Eric. Again, my apologies."

"Take some of those pills I sent you. They'll calm your nerves and help with your back and burn pains."

His stomach heaved into several knots. Valen's heart was pounding, as well as his ears. "I will, but first give me the driver's number that you hired. What was his name?"

"Wait a minute."

There was a pause as Valen's hand went through the clutter in a desk drawer until he found a pen. "Eric?"

"Got it, Valen. It's 555-8923. Area code 325." Valen repeated the number back to Eric Brannett, thanked him quickly, and hung up the phone to leave Eric to his girlfriend.

For more than an hour after, Valen paced his office floor, gripping Jesu's phone number in his hand. Finally, he realized he couldn't wait until the sun woke America to find out the answers to his questions. He didn't care about the driver. What the hell was stopping him from calling? Maybe he didn't want the answers?

He slowly dialed Jesu's number, letting it ring until finally a man answered.

"Hello."

"Is this Jesu, the limousine driver hired to drive Angel Frederick?"

"Yes, Sir." Jesu gasped. "Is this Valentino?"

"This is Valen. You drove my fiancée from the private airport in Madison to a friend's house in Pinon. Tell me where you dropped her off, what hotel?"

He did follow Angel's instruction for now. "Ridgemont." She did pay him well. "West side of Pinon."

"Ridgemont, that is a Bed and Breakfast with no phones." Valen remembered from his list. "She would not usually stay where there is no usable phone."

"Sir, it's just a one-bedroom garage out of a couple's house. I believe it to be safe."

Valen's voice turned instantly harsh. "I don't believe you! Where is she?"

"That is where I took her."

Valen knew his game. "I am willing to pay $50,000 dollars to the person who tells me exactly where I can find my future wife at this very minute!"

Silence.

"Sir, I could tell you another location she might have mentioned, let's say for $75,000 dollars in cash and permanent employment as your personal driver."

Valen approved of his gall. "That is a bold request." There was a long pause while Valen tried to calm his temper. "Not many have found me at such a loss."

"Then I have your word, Valen, that you will allow me the chance to further myself, to prove how great an employee I can really be."

"A man is only as good as his word."

Jesu cracked a grin, knowing the irony.

"Now, tell me where my fiancée is, before my patience grows thin."

* * * *

Valen was outside the hotel room when Angel ran out. He had seen everything, even their dancing in the club. His brown eyes were glaring through the open door at Jack, full of hate. "Come outside."

Angel ran back to Jack. "Valen, there is no reason to hurt Jack. Nothing happened between us."

"Get him."

Through the open windows and from the connecting inside door several men rushed into the room. All of them grabbed Jack, before he had time to react.

"Valen, please," Angel begged.

Valen ignored the plea and pushed her out of the way. "Make him stand."

Immediately, Jack began to resist as Valen's men began pulling and shoving him upward. He kicked one man in the stomach, taking him down. But five remained holding and punching Jack until he was forced to stand in front of Valentino, bleeding from the nose and mouth.

"I saw how you touched Angel in the club."

"Go to hell, Valen!" Jack spit.

Valen tightened a gloved hand and punched Jack in the face with a mighty thrust. "I suggest you treat me with respect considering the circumstances."

"I've given you plenty of respect over the years." Valen simply said, "Consider yourself fired."

Jack wheezed in pain. "I quit yesterday, the moment you walked out on Angel."

"I've changed my mind concerning her." Valen's left temple started to tick in a fast, violent rhythm. "I missed her."

"Maybe she's changed her mind about you!" Jack's features-built physique and short white-blond hair were now dripping with blood.

"Release this idiot and go."

Valen's men exited the bedroom the moment they were ordered, leaving Valen alone with Jack, and one hysterical woman, crying for Valen to stop.

"I have news for you, Jack." Valen instantly moved forward. "Angel is mine." Quickly he punched Jack in the stomach, causing Jack to drop to the floor.

Jack somehow managed to find the strength to get halfway back on his feet and clutched one hand into a fist. He lunged at Valen.

Suddenly, Eric Brannett rushed into the room, pulled out a gun. "I wouldn't even think of touching one hair on Valen's head."

Valen raised a hand for Eric to leave. "I can handle him."

"Wait," Jack said through clenched teeth, "until I tell the guards, Eric, about what I learned in…"

Three gunshots filled the room with screeching death calls. The first was fatal and exploded through Jack's heart, the second pierced the center of his brain, and the third, sliced and severed his groin. Blood was in every corner, on every wall, and now seeping even into the carpet of the hotel room floor.

Valen, smelling the death that Eric Brannett had just caused, grabbed Angel. He grasped her firmly and pulled her out of the room into the bathroom.

Angel screamed over and over: "No! No!"

"Look at what your whore made me do!" Eric Brannett roared. "She made me kill a guard to keep our interest's secret. Jack knew way too much."

Angel begged Valen. "Please, don't let him kill me." In Valen's arms, she fainted onto the bathroom floor.

A whisper called to her from the shadows. "Sexy, please wake up. I'm all right. Forgive yourself." Jack? Was that his voice coming from the darkness? She tried to see Jack's dead body but then she realized she wasn't on the cold, hard tile floor anymore.

Tenderly a hand was stroking her hair. She felt it lovingly caress her cheek. Her arms reached up to touch the man comforting her. Was Jack still alive? Was it possible?

"Wake up."

Her eyes began to flutter open.

Jono was sitting beside her in the guest bedroom at the Haze ranch. "Angel, you're having a nightmare. Wake up."

CHAPTER 15

Angel sat up, her raven curls falling down around her shoulders as she pulled back the bed covers to look at him. "Jono, what are you doing here?"

"You were having a nightmare. I came in to make sure you were okay." She felt the blush rise to her cheeks.

"Did I wake you?"

"No, I wake with the sun."

He was bare-chested. His rippled muscles were still moist from a shower. The hat she had bought him was on his head, pushing down his short, spiked hair. She wanted to run her fingers down every water droplet and smooth the moisture from his hair. "I'm sorry to have bothered you."

Jono leaned down and kissed her cheek. "I'm glad it was only a bad dream."

Angel's heart pounded, feeling the heat from his face.

"It's time to start getting ready for my grandmother's birthday party. Guests will be coming soon." Then he rose, took another look at her lying in bed, and left, shutting the door behind him.

* * * *

The home was filled with voices coming from downstairs. Angel stood in front of a mirror in a flowered Princess styled dress she had brought especially for the party. It was simple and eloquent with pink and yellow rose print and pink high heels to match.

Toward the end of the guest bedroom, a smaller mirror hung on the back of the wooden door. She crossed to it and began brushing out the tangles in her long raven hair. She had makeup but decided to go for the more natural look.

A knock at the door suddenly startled her. "Yes?"

"Angel, you ready?"

She recognized Jono's deep voice and opened the door. "I'll be right down."

Jono's big blue eyes widened. "You look very lovely this morning."

He was now wearing black jeans and a matching button-down shirt. A tan bandanna hung around his neck along with his golden cross. "So do you."

Then he added, removing his cowboy hat with one hand, "Not that you don't look this lovely every day."

"I take it everyone's here now?" she asked.

"Most of the family is here. They've all been looking forward to meeting you. I guess my grandmother has been doing a lot of talking about you."

Her hands trembled as she smoothed her dress. "I'm so nervous."

"Don't be." Jono smiled. "My family will love you as much as I do."

* * * *

Below, Mrs. Haze was in the kitchen in front of a huge white rectangular birthday cake with a large number of lighted candles on top. Thirty or more men, women and children were packed into the tiny living room, adjacent kitchen and porch, singing, "Happy Birthday to you, Happy Birthday to you…"

One by one every eye, including Mrs. Haze's turned toward the couple descending the wooden stairs.

Angel began to sing enthusiastically with the rest of them, but Jono didn't. Instead, his arm wrapped around her shoulders until the song ended with applause. Just as his grandmother prepared to blow out the candles, Mrs. Haze closed her eyes and made a wish.

As soon as the clapping ended, a man approached them. Angel recognized him instantly by his long black hair, brownish skin and strikingly handsome features.

"Angel," LaFordge greeted.

Jono froze then whispered in LaFordge's ear something Angel could not hear.

"Don't worry, Brother, everything's taken care of. No one will mention your special talents today."

"Thank you."

"After the party, however, we need to discuss what you need to do about Whitefeather."

"Agreed."

"Hello, my name's Nikky." Angel turned to find a lovely young woman standing behind her. She was tall, pretty with reddish-brown hair and a perfect dimpled smile.

"Hi, I'm Angel."

"Jono's told us about you." Nikky waved to a child across the room. "That's my son, Christopher. Would you like to meet him?"

For the next few minutes, Angel conversed with the child and immediately adored him.

"Call me, Chris," the boy said, and then he turned toward Nikky. "Momma, can I go wrestle with Uncle LaFordge?"

"Sure."

Angel watched the child burst out the door and saw LaFordge tackling him outside. She was moved by LaFordge's tenderness. There was a side to him she realized she hadn't yet seen.

Nikky pointed to three attractive women standing beside Jono's grandmother. "These are Jono's other sisters."

Angel smiled. "It's wonderful to meet you all."

"The one wearing the jeans and the cowboy hat is Meryl," Nikky announced. "She's the oldest, but don't ever tell her that. She'll deny it." Meryl's hair was the color of sunshine. She was thin and well built. Her eyes were as blue as Jono's and she seemed to carry herself with the same kind of confidence.

"Meryl doesn't look old at all." Angel laughed. "She's stunning." "Tonis, the one on the end," Nikky added, "is the next to oldest."

Tonis was smiling as Angel glanced her way. She was darker than the other sisters with cinnamon colored hair and dark brown eyes. She appeared more like a Native American compared to the other siblings with her more prominent cheek bones and higher forehead.

Tonis was lovely, Angel thought, as she returned the smile. "The one in the center is Martha."

Angel couldn't help but to catch the hint of jealousy in Nikky's voice as she introduced Martha. And to see Martha, it was easily understood why. Martha had long blonde hair, golden brown eyes and a figure most women would kill for. She looked more like a model than a cowgirl to Angel. In fact, Angel couldn't even picture such a beautiful woman straddling a horse and dirtying her clothes.

"She's the gorgeous one," Tonis remarked.

"Yes, everyone says so," Nikky agreed, "but I think we all are."

Angel nodded in agreement. "Is Jono's mother here?" Angel began searching the room for a woman who looked like Jono and Angel found her. In the corner of the kitchen was a woman—Angel would have known as Jono's mother anywhere. She was sandy haired with big blue eyes and the same dimpled smile.

"That's her." Nikky noticed Angel staring. "And the tall man behind her is my father." There was a twinkle in her father's eyes as he was talking with their mother.

"They really have something special, don't they?" Angel commented.

"Yes," Nikky agreed. "We are quite the attractive folk. We are very blessed to be so close. What's your family like?"

"I don't really have a family. Most of my family have passed away or moved out of my life in some way or another."

Nikky sensed her loneliness. "I'm sorry."

Angel sighed. "That's very kind of you to care."

"I'm hoping we'll become the best of friends," Nikky said.

"I hope so, too."

"Come on, Angel," Jono's grandmother suddenly called for her. "Jono, help me cut this cake so I don't have to stare at all these starving people anymore."

The crowd instantly moved to the sides to let both of them through to the table. The men tapped their cowboy hats in admiration, and to Jono they nodded with respect.

"How can your family and friends eat cake first thing in the morning?" Angel asked as she reached for the knife on the kitchen table and began cutting pieces.

He gazed into her eyes and it took him several seconds before he decided to answer. "Not just cake, there's a pig roasting out back, country fried steak, eggs, sausage, and chicken." Then he smiled brilliantly. "The chicken's for you."

"But I don't usually eat breakfast."

"That's fine. People will be coming in and out all day. Those who are already here know that the gettin' is good if you come early. Cake is the first thing to go, even this early in the morning."

"You won't be leaving after you eat, will you?"

He smiled. "No, I got a neighbor to overlook my ranch hands today, since it's my grandmother's birthday."

"That was nice of him." Angel lifted up a large piece of chocolate cake. "Is this big enough for a man your size."

"Big enough for my first round."

She opened her mouth in disbelief. "First round?"

"Sometimes I eat three." Angel closed her gaping mouth, turned around and began handing out plates of cake to the guests with a warm smile.

"It takes a lot of cake to support a body my size," Jono said.

Conversation was growing louder as many of the guests were eating, drinking, shaking hands and talking among themselves. Angel went around the table and began circulating soon after she had finished serving.

"Aren't you coming, Jono?" Angel invited him to join her and Nikky.

"It would be my pleasure."

Throughout the day, Angel moved from person to person making pleasant conversation Angel often brought Jono into the conversation to get his opinion. Once, she even placed her hand on his arm and leaned in to hear his every word.

"Is that your second country fried steak or is that my imagination?" Angel giggled.

"Yes, my second." He held out a forked piece of medium-well cooked meat. "Would you like a taste?"

"I think I'll stick to the barbeque chicken."

"That's fine, just be sure you tell my sister, Meryl, you just don't eat beef. I would hate for her to be insulted because you didn't eat what she prepared." Jono pointed to his sister who was surrounded by cowboys. "She brings practically a herd's worth of hamburgers, every year."

"Sure." Angel moved toward her. Jono caught her hand, wanting her to stay a few seconds longer.

"Have I told you, Angel, you're the sweetest thing, I've ever met?" He leaned down and warmly kissed her hand.

No one but her own mother had ever given Angel a compliment about anything other than her singing voice or her appearance before. Angel took a deep breath as his compliment tugged at her heart strings. "Why do you say that?"

"Just the way you are. Everyone seems to be able to open up to you."

"Everyone likes you, too."

"Everyone expects a lot out of me." Jono smiled. "I have certain talents."

"Angel," Meryl called from the porch. "Come here, you have to see Chris wrestling LaFordge."

"Excuse me." Angel rushed past him to see. Once she reached Meryl's side, she gazed at LaFordge pretending to be pinned by Chris' wrestling.

"It looks like Chris is winning!" Angel laughed, knowing LaFordge was letting him win.

Meryl winked to her then shouted, "See, Chris, you can do it. LaFordge is nothing compared to you."

From the corner of her eye, Angel saw a man coming on horseback. She knew he was related to Jono before Meryl announced his arrival. "That's my brother, Littlebear. He's nicknamed, the Bear," Meryl said.

He was slightly smaller in height, but he had the same cocky grin and brute appealing features as Jono. His hair was long and sandy. He was dressed in blue jeans and a white shirt clung to his brawny frame.

Jono came up behind Angel. "That's Bear."

"Yes, your sister was telling me."

"Would you like to meet him?"

"Sure, but I'd like to talk with Martha first if you don't mind. Her husband's a cop, isn't that what you told me?"

"Yes," Jono said.

"They make a very cute couple," Angel said.

Jono greeted his younger brother who dismounted and tied his horse to a fence. "Hey, Bear. Are you upset with me for supporting Whitefeather?"

"If you want to respect a doctor who has no respect for our culture, then yes, I am upset with you. Because of our father, we are Native American or have you forgotten that?"

"Can't we argue about this after the birthday party?" Bear grinned devilishly.

"I suppose."

Angel walked inside the house and began talking to Tonis. When the three brothers walked in, all eyes turned to them. Angel couldn't help but notice all the women heading their way. "Having fun?" Jono went to stand by Angel's side.

Bear followed him and asked, "So you are Angel?"

Angel couldn't help noticing that Bear had the same solid jawline as Jono. "Yes." She held out her hand for him to shake.

Bear bent down and kissed her hand. "She's perfect for you, Jono."

"Yes, she is perfect." Angel lowered her lashes. Her cheeks were on fire from Jono's compliment.

"Is there a wedding in the future?" Bear chuckled.

Jono wrapped Angel into his massive arms, giving her a loving hug. "If she would marry me, Brother, I'd be the happiest man alive."

Suddenly, the room burst into a loud cheer. Angel whirled her head around to find all the townspeople and Jono's family hooting and whistling for them.

Jono released her. The crowd stopped cheering the moment he spoke. "Mind your own business."

The rest of the day went well. Angel enjoyed herself. She felt as if she had known this family her entire life. She even listened to their gossip about their favorite bulls and what their brands looked like.

Jono's grandmother had long ago fallen asleep, but he was more than satisfied with her reaction to his and Angel's presents this afternoon. She did just as he had thought, told Angel she had spent too much on the sewing table. But then Angel kissed her and told her she would give her the world if she could; it made his grandmother cry loving tears.

They were just like mother and daughter the way they related. This day had brought them closer together, just as he had dreamed. The most important people in Jono's life were under the same roof, the roof he had built with his bare hands, and he was loving every minute of it. He made his way through the last of the crowd.

"Looks like people are leaving, Angel, because the sun is starting to set." He stood by her, looking out to the changing colors of the darkening sky.

"Yes," she admitted, sadly. Then she smiled up at him. "I've never had such a glorious day."

"I'm glad."

"Your family is wonderful."

A cowboy cut in, removing his hat for Angel. "We all must be going back to the Phillips' ranch, Ma'am, but we sure had a grand time getting to know you." He glanced up at Jono. "Thank you for letting us come and celebrate Grace's birthday." Then he turned and left with a group of men following him out of the front porch.

Angel gasped. "That was the last of your guests."

"Oh, don't worry. When Nikki has her baby in eight months, there's going to be just as big a celebration and you'll of course be invited."

"She's pregnant! How wonderful." Angel glanced back through the door. "This day has gone by so fast. I won't even be able to say goodbye to Daisy and Bill now. My driver will be here soon, so I won't miss my eight o'clock flight back to New York tonight."

Jono reached out and took her by both hands, pulling her body to his. "Angel."

"What is it?" She glanced up into his big blue eyes.

"Please stay another night."

"I can't."

"Take a later flight then. I have to go to Bear's for a short meeting then I'll be back. I don't want you to leave without us getting a chance to say goodbye."

Angel felt so drawn to him, she couldn't help but to stand on her tippy- toes and kiss him gently on the lips. "All right, but I have to leave tonight."

CHAPTER 16

"How was your meeting with Bear?"

Jono knelt beside the rocking chair on the front porch. "As well as can be expected."

"My driver is late."

The coldness in her voice made him stiffen. "You sound upset about his tardiness."

Angel continued to rock in one of the porch's rocking chairs. "I have to get home."

"To Valen?" Jono said. "What hold does he have over you? You don't love him."

"I do love him."

"If you loved him, you wouldn't look at me the way you do."

"It's a different kind of attraction."

"Angel, you're not angry with me. There's no reason to explain. I'm the one you were meant to be with."

"You arrogant…" Angel stifled the name calling. Jono was the farthest thing from arrogant and she knew it. He only spoke what he felt in his heart. His eyes were dancing with their brilliant blue fire, and then he grinned.

"You don't think that."

"Stop looking so smug."

He chuckled lightly. "You're angry at yourself now because you've fallen in love with another man."

"We can only be friends. Accept that."

"How can you stay engaged to a man you wish was me?"

"I do care very deeply for Valen. Other than a few problems, we're made for…" She couldn't say it.

"You can't lie to me, can you?" Jono leaned back on one elbow, gazing into her eyes. "You're not made for this other man, are you?"

"Jono, please. I can't deal with this right now. My driver's late and you have no idea how angry Valen will be if I don't check in."

Jono smiled. "Just tell me you're not in any danger staying with this Valen."

Angel scoffed. "How dare you even think that I'm in some kind of danger? You don't understand anything about what we have been through."

Jono sighed. "You're right. I do know that I haven't ever felt this way about a woman before. I don't know exactly what to say to get you to leave him."

"Then don't say anything else."

"I don't know quite what to say, because I've never been with a woman."

Angel slowly stood beside him as his words sunk into her brain. She tried her best to pretend not to be shocked by leaving her face expressionless, but she needed to know. "Did you just admit to being a virgin?"

"Yes, I suppose I did, Ma'am."

"I don't believe you. Look at you!" Angel said.

"I've always felt that I would share that experience with the woman I made my wife."

She thought for a moment what it would be like and then decided to quickly change the subject. "Thank you for telling me. Friends shouldn't keep secrets from one another."

Jono raised a brow. "We are friends, aren't we?"

"Yes." Angel swallowed hard, still taking in the enormity of his confession. "I'm very proud of that." It took all her strength just to sit next to him and not reach out and be embraced inside his loving arms.

Jono was a virgin just like her? He was a gorgeous man who loved her and wanted to marry her? He wanted to give this gift to her? There wasn't a treasure more valuable on earth!

How could Jono be so masculine and a virgin to boot! Didn't he know that made him even more irresistible? He was becoming her one temptation. And she too, had to do what was right and honorable.

"Being your friend, Angel, that means that you shouldn't keep any secrets from me either." Jono leaned down closer to her. Their eyes were locking. "Tell me how you really feel about me. Tell me how you really feel about this other man."

"I did."

His closeness was having an intense effect on her. Her senses tingled with his soft leather scent that robbed her of control.

What the hell did he want from her? "I have never been with a man that way either. I'm engaged to Valen. I'm going to marry him."

"Angel, I deserve to know everything. I deserve to know at least why you're marrying another man when I'm the one you want." Jono's eyes showed their first signs of weakness, their first signs of desperation.

Angel couldn't tell Jono about Jack's murder, or that if she left Valen what Eric Brannett might do to her to keep the murder a secret. Valen needed her. After all he'd been through, he was the one that had saved her from living on the streets. He'd always been there for her.

Angel racked her brain for something to tell Jono, even if it was a lie. She had to, this time. The lie was justifiable for Jono's own safety and for the health of Valen.

A thought, an idea came to her. It was a lie, a lie that would change everything, change how Jono felt for her. It would stop his questions for good… and his advances. "Valen can give me things you can't and couldn't ever," Angel said in haste, before she could change her mind.

"Like what?" Jono took a deep breath, afraid of what he was about to hear.

"He built my singing career into a multi-million dollar a year business. He provides mansions around the world, cars, money, designer clothes, everything a woman could ever want." She smiled dramatically for further effect. "He flies me all around the world in his private jets." She swallowed hard, watching Jono turn his head away from her. "I've got bank accounts already for my unborn children. I can go where I want, when I want, all over the world. He has made me what I am today. My pictures are in every music magazine!"

Angel blinked away her tears. "He can give me things you can't and couldn't ever supply. That is why I must marry Valen and not you."

With every blasphemous word from her lips, Angel ripped Jono's heart into shreds. She saw the pain come across his face and his eyes turned away from her. Her protective lies crushed and destroyed him just as Angel had known they would. Jono now believed he could not make her happy. "I'm sorry, Jono, but that is all I want out of a husband."

"I can only provide wealth of the heart." He stood and walked through the open porch door. "If that's not enough, then this other man is more of what you need."

"I am sorry to have to tell you these things."

Jono swung on his beloved hat. "I don't know why you are lying to me. You love me more than any of those things. You're lying, maybe to protect me from something." He headed out into the field. "We'll talk about this later, when you're willing to trust me. For now, I'll feed Wildshot. I'll be back shortly."

Angel did love him. She knew it with all her heart. She didn't know when she fell in love since they'd only known each other a short time. All she knew was loving Jono was pointless when a relationship between them could never happen.

Jono would make the perfect husband, yes, and the perfect father. When he was angry, he did his best to communicate with honesty and loyalty to find a solution that suited both of them. He was certainly easy on the eyes. But loving Jono was only a dream and a nightmare. He'd come too late in her life for Angel to change her mind on whom to marry.

She must marry Valen, for him, for her, so that they could have a future. Even though Valen wasn't Jono, he had history with her, a past of dependability. He had been the one man who had been there for Angel since her parents' death. It was he, and he alone who graciously took her off the streets and loved her as part of his family. He'd given her a career, a home, a reason for being happy for so many years.

Her feelings for Jono, because of hers and Valen's past, were simply irrelevant. Her fate had already been determined. She was going to marry Valen and somehow learn to deal with the consequences.

She owed Valen. She was his lifeline to happiness. "Where's Jono, Deary?" Angel hadn't heard Mrs. Haze calling for her, or Mrs. Haze wheeling herself into the porch.

After several minutes, Mrs. Haze repeated, "Where's Jono?" Angel's gaze rose from being lowered.

"He's with Wildshot." The room again darkened with silence.

"I see. It's getting colder, Deary; why don't you come inside the house and sit until he returns?"

"All right."

Mrs. Haze couldn't help but wonder what had occurred while she was asleep. Angel seemed too distant and withdrawn as she crossed into the house and sat on the sofa. "Did something happen between you two, something I should know about?"

When Angel didn't answer, Mrs. Haze then added, "You know, Deary. You can tell me anything."

Guilt made her yearn to confess. "I kept something from Jono, Mrs. Haze. I had to. He wouldn't stop asking certain questions."

"I suppose he just had been asking you why you intend to marry another man when you love him instead."

"Yes."

Mrs. Haze harrumphed. "My grandson needs a reminder of how to respect a woman's privacy."

Angel disagreed. "No, what he does deserve is an answer. I just couldn't give him one he wants to hear."

"Or maybe one that you wanted to hear."

"I can't ever marry your son." Angel stiffened. "Why should I tell him how I feel and then break his heart?"

"I think that's already been done, Deary."

"What am I supposed to do? I'm helplessly in love and engaged to the wrong man."

"Wrong man?"

"I can't explain it." Angel tried to fight the knot beginning to tighten in her throat. "All I can say, is, I've never loved anyone like Jono before. I can't even believe love exists like this."

"That's wonderful."

"No, it's not. It's dangerous for me to love him." In her mind's eye, Angel pictured Jack, lying dead in a pool of blood. His eyes were haunted, opened wide and his face was beaten. Blood was still pouring out of the bullet holes from the center of his brain and his groin.

She could still smell the blood even though it was only a memory. It was as if Jack was right there, next to her, a reminder that staying with Valen kept her surrounded by dangerous people all protecting their own interests.

Even the feelings sometimes came flooding back, the guilt of not finding some way to stop Eric Brannett from murdering, the helplessness, the agony, the fear.

"What do you mean it's dangerous for you to love my grandson?"

Angel had revealed a secret too many. "It is just how I feel, that's all. I didn't mean dangerous, literally, Mrs. Haze."

"Oh." Mrs. Haze shifted in her wheelchair. "Are you sure?"

"Of course, I'm sure. Why would it be dangerous for me to love Jono?"

"You spoke of this other man."

"Mrs. Haze, I must be going. I can't believe how late my driver is." Angel pretended to notice the time on the kitchen clock, by glancing away.

"I think you're avoiding what I was just about to ask."

Angel realized every moment she stayed in Madison was a moment that she placed both Mrs. Haze and Jono in danger.

"No, of course not. I just have to hurry, that's all, and get my things before my limousine arrives."

"I will miss you."

Angel's heart had grown too fond; her feelings had grown too strong for Jono, for Mrs. Haze and for this haven inside this family-friendly western town. "I will miss you, too."

"When will you be coming back?"

"I won't ever be coming back." Angel gazed at the elderly woman who reminded her so much of her own mother, by her strength, by the love that flowed unconditionally from her, like a river to the oceans.

Tears came into Mrs. Haze's eyes. "I see. Well, whatever you think is best. I suppose it is."

"It's the best and safest thing for everyone."

Mrs. Haze turned her head away toward the open front door. "I think it might be already too late for safety."

Angel had been too caught up in her own tragic situation to have heard the limousine pulling up in front of the gardens and the man's heavy footsteps coming toward the house.

She raised her head and caught a glimpse of the figure coming in from the shadows. Tall, broad with hair as black as midnight, he was dressed to match the night in a dark tailored suit.

"Valen?" Caught like a mouse in a trap, Angel squealed out his name and rose to her feet.

"Hello, Principessa. I've come to visit with Bill and Daisy. Wasn't it strange, though? For some reason I had thought they were staying in Pinon, not Madison." Slowly Valen moved onto the porch and into the filtered light.

"I just wanted to visit the woman who had helped me after my car accident." Angel inched a frightened step backwards. "Remember, Mrs.

Haze? I just wanted to wish her a happy birthday before flying back home." He entered the ranch's living room. Slowly, he came toward her, step by pounding step, until he stood in front of her.

"I do not know a Mrs. Haze, nor did I give you permission to be anywhere but Pinon," Valen roared.

"I'm Mrs. Haze. Welcome to my home." The woman in the wheelchair spoke up, letting him know they were not alone. "You just missed my birthday party. You must be a friend of Angel's."

Valen glared immediately over his shoulder to the woman.

"Hello," she greeted him a sweet tone. "Would you like a piece of my birthday cake? You are in luck. This year there is actually one piece left."

CHAPTER 17

alen's eyes widened, gawking at the woman below in the wheelchair, smiling up at him. She appeared as a ghost, a ghost from his past. "She looks like your Madre?"

Angel circled around Valen, grateful that he wasn't as upset as she had thought he might be.

"Yes, Valen, doesn't she remind you of my mother?"

"Yes, there is a resemblance, from all the pictures I've seen when your mother was in school, the way she does her hair and the same nose, I think. You miss your mother, dearly, even now."

"My apologizes, Mrs. Haze. I see that I caused the man I'm engaged to some worries by coming to your birthday party today," Angel said.

Valen crossed the room and kissed Mrs. Haze's hand. "Please forgive my rude intrusion."

"I will not hold a grudge, Mr…"

"Call me Valen. It's short for Valentino." He directly kept his gaze on Mrs. Haze's dark eyes. "It's an honor to meet any friend of Angel's." Valen lowered her hand, returning it to the wheelchair's arm.

Angel tried to stop herself from shaking involuntarily. "Can you understand, Valen, why I returned to this beautiful ranch?"

"Of course." Valen pivoted and affably strutted to Angel for a private conversation. He leaned over and whispered in her ear. "There is no reason to clarify your actions, Principessa."

"Great. Mrs. Haze and I were having a wonderful time."

"I only came," he pushed an unruly raven curl away from her ear, still sensing her fear, "because I had heard you were seen with a man in front of a local store here and purchased this man a hat."

"The man thought I was working for someone named Whitefather. Oh, it's such a long story!" Angel stretched the truth to save Jono from Valen's knowledge. "Oh, how could you question me after what happened to Jack?"

"My apologies, Principessa. I understood why you returned to Madison the moment I saw her."

"I would have told you everything. But I didn't think you'd understand how much it meant to me to have her as a friend."

"Shh, don't worry, Principessa." Before she could finish scolding him, his left hand rose and went through his straight black hair in one frustrated movement.

Angel noticed the bandage on his hand. "Does your hand still hurt?"

Valen displayed a wicked grin. "You haven't seen it since it's been stitched. Have you?"

"No, is your hand going to be all right?"

"Get your things, Principessa. You've stayed away from me too long." Angel nodded and rushed up the stairs. She didn't want to leave the Haze Ranch. But she knew the moment Valen shattered this home's serenity, she had made the right decision. She must leave the Haze ranch to protect both Jono and Mrs. Haze.

She grabbed her purse from off the bed, gave the tiny bedroom one last look then came rushing down the wooden stairs to Mrs. Haze's side.

"I must be leaving now," she whispered woefully in Mrs. Haze's ear, giving her a warm hug. "Please, don't worry. I'll be fine."

Mrs. Haze smiled as if understanding. "Take care, Deary. I love you like a daughter, always remember."

Angel hugged her again as Valen came from behind and snatched one of her arms. "Time to go, Principessa."

She let him escort her out of the home even though her desire was never to leave this little piece of heaven on earth.

With every beat of her heart, with every breath granted to her by God, Angel knew she would never forget how much she loved this ranch and these two people who had made this sanctuary so special.

Mrs. Haze always made a point to make her feel appreciated. Talking to her was like talking to a friend Angel had known all her life. She was able to open up to her like a mother and tell her things that normally she would never be able to tell another living person.

Jono made her feel alive! Every time spent with him, she'd been enveloped by his love and his attempts to make developmental steps to bring their relationship closer. He'd showed her how much she meant to him. Ever since he'd pulled her from the wrecked car and comforted her from her fears of the storm, Angel had treasured his sensitivity.

Leaving them, leaving this ranch, and knowing she may never be able to visit them or this place again, broke her heart. It was in everyone's best interest for her to leave, and never return, but acknowledging it didn't make the pain hurt any less.

She loved them. Even as Valen led her toward the limousine, she knew that she would forever miss them and this place.

There was a certain peace here in Madison, as far as her eyes could see over the flat lands and the swaying tall grasses. In everything, she could hear crickets, frogs; their lives seemed a nirvana away from the bustle of the city.

Jesu, the skinny blond-haired young man, opened the door for her. "Ms. Frederick."

"Goodbye, Deary!" Mrs. Haze yelled from the porch.

Angel didn't reply. As she slinked past Jesu, she was preoccupied with giving him a glare that would have killed, if looks were deadly. She knew he'd told Valen where she was.

"She said goodbye to you, Principessa."

Angel turned and waved goodbye, fighting back her tears and the need to run back into Mrs. Haze's arms.

"Get in the car. You're making a spectacle out of yourself. We have no time for emotional nonsense tonight."

Angel lowered herself into the limousine and scooted over, making room for him as he coldly seated himself beside her.

Jesu shut the limousine door. "Forget her, Principessa."

Angel glared up at him, but Valen's attention was drawn outside of the car window to the barn, behind the house. "Valen!" she called, instantly realizing that at any moment Jono could come walking out of the barn and Valen would spot him if she didn't gain his attention. "I'm sorry for upsetting you."

"I don't want you to come here again." Angel's heart cringed. "Promise me, you will not return."

Angel couldn't; instead, she evaded answering. "Are you so mad at me that you'd rather order me about then grant me a warm embrace?"

"I don't feel much like holding you, Principessa. You should have called and told me you were coming here."

"I tried." Angel straightened. "I was going to tell you, but you were very short with me on the phone. I guessed that you wouldn't allow me to come."

"You were right." Valen leaned sideways, back toward her and gave a long, dragged-out sigh. "I wouldn't have let you come at all."

"How can I be completely honest with you, Valen, if you don't grant me any freedom?"

"I hurt every time I do not know where you are. Do you understand that? It kills me. I feel like a trapped animal until I know that you are safe and that everything is okay. It's hard enough for me to go on these business trips without you. The least you can do is stay where you are supposed to stay, and answer your phone, bloody hell!"

"Okay, Valen, don't get angry."

"It's the least you can do." His chiseled face turned as his gaze drifted upward. "All that matters, Principessa, is that you're with me."

Over Valen's shoulder, Angel caught a glimpse of a figure coming out of the barn. The figure one-handedly retrieved a pitchfork stuck in the ground by the barn's door, then returned inside the building, not noticing the limousine parked by the side of the house.

Fearfully, Angel looked to Valen, whose gaze had not moved from an upward direction. "Thank God."

"Pardon?" Valen hadn't heard what she mumbled.

"When is this limousine going to move?" Angel inquired matter-of-factly, not to cause Valen to become suspicious. "It seems like we've been sitting here an hour or so."

Valen was pleased that Angel desired to leave. He lowered the driver's window between them by the switch on the limousine door. "Jesu, take us to the airport."

Jesu had been hoping Valen had witnessed the big husky cowboy grabbing for the pitchfork a few seconds ago. Unfortunately for him, Valen hadn't. "Yes, Sir, but I do have to check the tires."

"I've had enough of your excuses and your stories, Jesu! I strongly suggest that you carry on. I don't want to miss our flight."

"What did he tell you, Valen, that I was sneaking off to be with some man?" Angel asked ostentatiously, knowing Jesu could hear.

Valen raised the window separating them. "I had no right to come here, Principessa, no matter who told me anything. I just had assumed, after hearing about your purchasing this man a hat; well, I'm sure you know why I came. It's not like you haven't fallen prey before to another man's whims. I was only trying to protect you. You know how I worry."

"Valen, there is no need to worry about me." Her gaze drifted to the left of his eyes and peered through the car window as the barn door in the distance was swung open by a gust of wind.

Inside, a man's large shadow cold be easily seen, pitching hay and flickering against the back of the barn wall.

Thinking instinctively, Angel laid her head hard on Valen's shoulder to draw all of his attention. "I've missed you, so."

Her skin felt so warm to him and so fragile in the darkness of the limousine. "I'm a lucky man to have such a forgiving, loving woman." He smiled dazzling down on her as the car engine started and the limousine began carrying the couple off into the Colorado night.

* * * *

An hour later, in the living room of the Haze house, Jono stood in front of his grandmother, sweat still on his brow. "Did she say where this man was taking her?"

Mrs. Haze wheeled herself to the house's front doorway to look out over the vegetable and sunflower gardens.

"Look at me and tell me where they were headed."

Mrs. Haze turned her wheelchair to face her grandson, the man who had saved at least one hundred men, even horses and property from their doom. She'd never seen him like this. Losing Angel, worrying for her safety had changed his confidence, even the way he stood. He was frightened. For the first time, Mrs. Haze saw fear lurking in her grandson's big blue eyes, fear, which could cause failure.

"I don't know where Angel is. But it doesn't matter. It's best you let her make her own choices on who she wants to be with. Valentino could be dangerous. I've seen his kind before."

Jono roared. "Angel wouldn't stay with a man who beats her. He can't be the man she says she's going to marry!"

"Something's wrong. She's either afraid of him or something back home. Leave them alone, Jono. I lost your grandfather. One dead in my family is enough!"

"I can't, not if she's not safe."

Mrs. Haze's dark eyes filled with caring tears and useless anger. "Didn't you hear me? I said, one dead in my family is enough. For a woman, that kind of man will kill, damn it. They'll kill to keep what they want to be theirs."

His grandmother hadn't said damn to him since he squashed her tomato plants when he was five. He acknowledged she was serious and distraught by sitting down at the kitchen table to give her more time to speak her piece.

"Even you can't help her," Mrs. Haze said, continuing to protest.

"I'll talk to Valentino. I'll get her away, my way! He won't have any reason for violence."

Her pudgy cheeks were a frustrated red. "Jono, he doesn't know you or your reputation. You talk to him. He'll laugh then strike you down." She began to weep. "Maybe she'll come back. I know she will. She'll come back and she'll be on our land. Madison folks will protect you because you're their hero, their 'Cowboy,' their legend."

Her tears banished any fury he might have had, hearing her use the nickname he loathed. "I'm nothing but a man."

"And a man is nothing but flesh and blood. I can't risk losing you. You leave after him, and you'll never come back. What will I do then?"

"I'll have someone here for you." He leaned closer to her, got down on one knee and held her hand. "One of the sisters will check on you while I'm gone."

"You're not listening to me. I can't lose you. Valentino will try to harm anything that tries to take Angel away! That's the kind of man he is. He got upset that she was even here. I know this just as I know my heart breaks for Angel and the life she's living."

Jono understood his grandmother's fears. "All men can be reasoned with, all men. Angel can't live like this. No woman, man or child deserves to be scared for their lives. I'm sorry, Grandmaw, but I've got to make sure Angel's all right. I'll try New York first at that address you kept in your Bible."

Mrs. Haze clutched his shirt sleeve until her weakened body could stand. "No."

"Trust me. Have faith."

"I only have faith in the Almighty."

"Then believe in Him, Grandmaw. The Bible says, 'I know the plans I have for you, plans for good and not harm, to give you a future with hope.'"

She wiped her eyes. "I love you, Jono."

"Wherever I go, He is with me and He's watching over me. You, too."

"What if she doesn't want to leave Valen, or won't tell you why she's acting so scared?"

"Then I'll be the one to go."

"And if she does want to come back with you?"

"Then I'll bring her home and wait for Valentino to follow."

CHAPTER 18

The short note she had sent by messenger repeated itself in his mind. Had that letter not arrived the moment when he was about to follow the limousine, he would have gone to New York after Angel.

Jono,

I'm so sorry that I didn't get a chance to say goodbye. My fiancé arrived, and I'm so happy to be with him and return home. Hope to see you soon. Please do not worry. I'll be counting the days until I can return to your ranch.

Your friend, Angel

* * * *

The sun was shining brightly when Jono dismounted off of Wildshot. He removed his beloved cowboy hat and let the sun's rays beat down upon his handsome face as he lowered his body to the hard ground.

He lay on top of Counsel Hill, flat on his back, to watch the clouds move northwest across the blue sky and to ponder.

Just another day, adding to the last several months that the Cowboy had been coming to this hill after work was done to be alone and think of Angel. He missed her. As more days passed by, he wondered if he hadn't made a mistake by not traveling to New York after her.

Since she'd been gone, he hadn't had a good night's sleep or been able to work to his full efficiency. Even now as his eyes closed and he covered his face with his broad-brimmed hat, sleep wouldn't come.

He was too frustrated. He hadn't been able to shake the disturbing feeling that Angel wasn't really all right and that was why she hadn't returned to Madison.

The note was proof Angel had left Madison of her own volition.

Some fearless hero, he was. Jono laughed silently. Word from her and he gave in, even though he knew with all of his heart that her choice was not in her best interest.

"Well," he decided, tossing off his snakeskin boots, "I'll give her one more month and then it's off to New York. That's the only way to learn if she's truly as happy as she claims to be. And to be able to get on with his life, if she is."

The "Cowboy" felt the approach of two horses from the west. By one of the horses' heavy, pounding left front hoof, the legend knew who the horses and riders were.

His brothers were coming.

The horse with the slightly injured leg was none other than Jennie. She was the mare Bear took in after she had become injured.

"Mornin'."

From underneath his cowboy hat, Jono greeted. "Mornin', Bear." LaFordge dismounted and squatted down next to Jono's resting body.

"We wanted to know why you did it."

"Did what?"

"You know what! Look me in the eye. We're trying to talk to you!" Jono didn't remove the hat from covering his face.

LaFordge flicked the hat off. "Now tell us why."

"I suppose your referring to my convincing Whitefeather to move his medical practice out off of Native American land and to the other side of Madison."

"We know you'd never agreed with our position."

"We didn't believe you'd change your mind," Bear pressed in agreement. "Especially after you told us you would have no part in closing down a legal business."

"I still don't agree with your efforts to destroy his practice especially when so many agree with his modern medicine. I sympathize with both sides in this, his and yours."

"Ours is right," LaFordge deemed.

Jono didn't reveal an inch of emotion. "I just explained to Whitefeather how the community felt that some of the locals didn't approve of his modern medicines. I simply explained to him that many of our Native Americans here show loyalty to their Shaman instead."

"And he took your advice to move his practice just outside of town." Bear grinned as only Bear could, brilliantly.

"I suppose, he did."

LaFordge picked up Jono's hat and pressed it back down on Jono's face. "Our Shaman went to Whitefeather's new office this morning and they smoked the peace pipe. Their war is over."

Jono tipped up his hat to find LaFordge mounting his stallion, ready to leave. "I don't like discord in Madison. Regardless of if I think you are right or wrong, LaFordge, you are my brother and I love you."

LaFordge turned his stallion around and was about to snap his reins. For a moment LaFordge waited, as if pondering how to respond. Then to the shock of both Jono and Bear, LaFordge mumbled, "Thank you, Brother. I feel the same."

Bear chuckled as LaFordge retreated. "That was almost impossible for him to admit."

"I know how he feels, even if he says nothing."

* * * *

"Valen, Daisy had her baby!" Angel burst into Eric Brannett's New York office. "Can I visit her and Mrs. Haze? I'd like to invite them to our wedding."

126

Valen and Brannett were sitting opposite each other in the black leather chairs in front of the large picture window that overlooked Central Park. Their heads turned the instant Angel rushed into the room.

"Angel." Eric Brannett stood.

"I'm sorry. I didn't realize that you two were still in a meeting."

Eric Brannett halfheartedly smiled at her and then slowly crossed the office to his door. "I will leave you two alone for privacy." He left, shutting the door behind him.

"Did I interrupt something important?"

"You didn't, Principessa. I upset Eric, long before you graced this office with your presence." Valen motioned her to come and sit next to him in the black leather chair opposite.

"Fine. I'm sorry to have bothered you." She began to rise to leave, trying to maintain her composure.

Valen captured her forearm. "This, Mrs. Haze, she means that much to you, to interrupt this meeting with Eric?"

"Yes."

"Why?" Valen showed her the chair and she sat down. "Do I need to say what you already know, Angel? I believe it's because she looks so much like your mother."

"Mrs. Haze is my friend. I care for her. I would like her to attend our wedding and I could even use her advice on my dress and even on some of the decorations."

"I can hire the best Event Planner in the world for that. What about your friend Dawn, isn't she going to be your Matron of Honor?"

"Yes. I thought you didn't like her, Valen."

"Isn't she out stomping on kittens and killing the Pope?"

"What?"

"Let big boobs Dawn help you instead."

Oh, how he pissed her nearly to tears! "Yes, maybe it is true that Mrs. Haze does remind me of my own mother. But it's my wedding, too. I should be able to have anyone there I want, no matter what my reasons are. Having Mrs. Haze attend our wedding would be like having my own mother there, and Dawn will make a fabulous Matron of Honor, too."

"Mrs. Haze is not your mother, Principessa."

"I know that, but I feel for her that way."

Valen took in a deep breath. "Fine, call me from Bill and Daisy's often and you must stay in the hotel room that I provide for you in Pinon. Jesu will drive you to the Haze ranch for a visit."

"Not Jesu!" Angel gasped.

"No matter who the driver is, you must stay in contact with me. Your driver can wait on the property," Valen said. "If you don't like Jesu, he'll be fired, and I'll find someone else."

"How long can my trip be?"

"Two days; you may go before you have that interview in California. Eric and I are trying to set that up today."

"Thank you, Valen, thank you!" Angel kissed him quickly on the cheek.

"Remember, Principessa, if you're not where you're supposed to be, I will be more than willing to come after you. And believe me, I… will… come after you."

"*Help!*"

CHAPTER 19

Eric Brannett heard a blood-curdling cry from the hallway and burst into his office to find Jesu standing over Valen who was lying on the floor. "What happened?"

Valen was twitching and convulsing over the carpet.

"Did you upset him?" Eric Brannett asked. "Did he take his pills?"

"No. He just collapsed."

"Help me lift him to the sofa," Eric Brannett ordered, and Jesu assisted Eric in carrying Valen's body onto the couch by the side of the desk.

"Valen tried to fire me, so I showed him a picture. He started fumbling for his jacket trying to get some kind of medicine bottle and then he just dropped," Jesu explained. "Is he having a seizure? Does he have epilepsy?"

"No, and his health is none of your concern."

"Should I call for an ambulance?" Jesu asked.

Eric Brannett kneeled down beside the couch. "Not yet."

Jesu backed away, continuing to watch Valen gripping at the leather couch. "What the hell is wrong with him?"

"There is nothing wrong with him." Eric Brannett's secretary suddenly entered and screamed.

"Calm down, Suzanne. They're both fine. Fetch me a glass of water."

"I should call an ambulance."

The agent opened the pill bottle on the floor. He turned it over and found it empty of any contents. "Get me Valen's other bottle of pills, Suzanne, and the water. Now!"

"Yes, Mr. Brannett." The woman left with her face turning as pale as Valen's.

"I wouldn't have shown him the picture, if I knew he had health problems."

Eric Brannett glared at Jesu behind him as he snapped his handkerchief out of his suit jacket and began wiping the sweat from Valen's face. "What picture?"

Jesu plucked the picture out of his jean pocket; the picture of Angel embracing the Madison cowboy in front of the convenience store and showed the picture to Eric Brannett.

The agent snarled and then agonizingly turned toward Valen as Valen grasped his jacket. "My pills!" Valen gasped.

Jesu returned the picture to his jeans.

Valen gasped out, his nails digging through his gloves and ripping holes into Eric Brannett's flesh. "Angel!"

"Valen, there's no reason for you to get upset. She's only giving some cowboy a hug."

Valen nodded. "It looks like they are about to kiss."

The secretary returned with another bottle of pills and a glass of water which was shaking in her hands. Eric Brannett took several pills out and handed Valen them to swallow. He did so, without water.

"Leave us, Suzanne. He'll be fine now," Eric Brannett ordered.

Valen took a few deep breaths and spoke. "I need to get off those things."

Eric Brannett crossed the floor and grabbed Jesu by the arm. "I'll be sure this man leaves you alone to rest! I'm sure it was only a hug, Valen. Angel wouldn't make the same mistake again like she did before. We both know what happened to Jack."

Valen grimaced. "You're right. She loves me now."

Dragging Jesu out of the office, Eric Brannett forced Jesu down a long corridor, around a bend and then pushed him into a vacant copy room. "What the hell were you trying to do?" He slammed the door hard and clutched Jesu by the front of his shirt.

"I didn't know Valen was ill."

"He's not." Eric Brannett protected Valen's image. "He was just late taking his medication."

Jesu dismissed. "What do you have him on? What are all those pills for?"

Eric Brannett released Jesu and took several steps back. "How did you acquire that worthless picture?"

"I took it the last time Angel was in Madison."

"I see."

"Since I wasn't rehired for this next trip, I thought if I proved what was going on, he'd want me to go back and make sure she never goes back to the ranch."

"Blackmail Valen, right? Is that what you might have tried to do to keep this all hush?"

Jesu wasn't ashamed. "I told him if he didn't give me a million dollars I would go to the press with it, expose her for the slut she is."

Eric Brannett suddenly smiled while moving his hand in then out from inside his jacket. "You're a fool."

Jesu opened the door and then suddenly closed it. "Why aren't you running to the phone to call the police? You want a cut?"

"We're already in business together, Jesu."

"Business?" Jesu found Eric Brannett grinning behind him.

"We're in the blackmail business. You were going to blackmail Valen, weren't you?" Jesu watched Eric Brannett lean against the copy machine and cross his arms.

"Now it's my turn. Take my jet, because you're going to Colorado tonight. You'll be Angel's driver. You're going to take more pictures, better ones. The picture you have now only implies she's cheating on Valen, it doesn't confirm it."

"Why do you want me to confirm it? Aren't you and Valen friends?"

"My friendship with Valen is none of your business."

"Why should I work for you?"

"I'll give you a job on my staff if you do well on this assignment."

"What kind of job?"

"Does it matter?" Eric Brannett shrugged away his inquiry. "If you don't go to Madison with Angel tonight on Valen's jet, I will call the police."

"So, you're blackmailing *me* now?"

Out from his hidden pocket in his suit jacket, Eric Brannett lifted a small voice activated tape recorder. Slowly, he rewound and played. "Blackmail Valen, right? Is that what you might have tried to do to keep this all hush?"

Jesu heard his own voice repeating itself. "I told him if he didn't give me a million dollars I would go to the press with it, expose her for the slut she is."

Eric Brannett pressed the top button and returned the tape recorder inside his jacket to be hidden again from view. "Funny, Jesu, after you spoke those words of confession, my tape recorder suddenly stopped recording. I'll tell you what. If you can prove that Angel is messing around with this cowboy, we'll forget this day ever happened, other than the day you get your due rewards. But if she's not having some fling in Madison, I suggest you stay the hell out of my sight."

"You'll call the police?"

"Better than that, Jesu, I'll give you a lesson you'll never forget: what blackmail is and how far you can take it before a man can snap."

"Is that what you did to Valen? I've heard rumors of someone named Jack. What happened to Jack?"

Eric Brannett laughed. "How naïve a young man like you can be, Jesu." He continued to chuckle. "You'll be lucky if you wind up like Valen by the time I get through with you, if you don't supply me with a much better picture."

"What are you planning to do with the photo when I return?"

"Something, Jesu, you should have thought of first."

* * * *

Too anxious to wait in her apartment, Angel went to the side of the street and waited on a bench for the limousine to take her to the airport.

Time seemed to pass too slowly. After fifteen minutes, she rose and began pacing in front of the bench until she heard the loud roar of a limousine engine coming toward her.

She grabbed her suitcase and then turned to find Jesu behind the wheel. "Good evening, Miss Frederick," Jesu greeted as he exited the vehicle with a cocky smile. "Your limousine has arrived."

Angel kept her head held high as Jesu laughed at her surprised expression and opened the back limousine door. "Good evening, Jesu, you're several hours late. Why was my flight rescheduled?"

"I was about to be fired, but something changed. I apologize for the delay. I had to take Eric Brannett's private jet to get here." Jesu smirked.

Angel bit her lip. "I had heard that you were getting fired tonight. What changed Valen's mind?"

"I can't disclose all that information." Jesu winked to her as she slowly lowered herself into the limousine with a sensual cross of her long silky legs. "All I can say is that you better be willing to pay a large sum to keep me from telling Valen about the Madison cowboy."

"I don't think so."

"I know so, because part of my orders were to keep an eye on you and make a full report of everyone you see and talk to in Madison."

"Why should I pay you a dime when you will just inform Valen of Jono anyway?"

"No, I wouldn't do that."

Angel gasped. "Why not, it's what you did last time I paid you?"

"I didn't break our verbal agreement. You paid me to keep my mouth shut and not mention the Madison cowboy."

"So instead, you just insinuate by showing Valen where I was staying."

"You should know I was loyal. I didn't tell Valen you spent the night with him or that he lives in the ranch we had visited."

"That's only because you wanted Valen to see for himself." Angel tried to slam the limousine door shut, but Jesu put his foot in the doorway.

"If I had really wanted Valen to know about Jono, wouldn't I have just driven the limousine closer to the barn? You know as well as I, the cowboy was inside pitching hay and feeding his horse." Jesu grinned. "I kept my word to both of you and kept the money."

"Scoundrel! Jono and I didn't even sleep together!"

Jesu pushed away Angel's hand that was trying to grasp the door handle. "I kept my word and I'll keep it again. This time just be more specific on what I am supposed to accomplish."

"I can't trust a man who only wants money."

"If you don't trust me, there will be quite an extensive write up about that cowboy in my report to Valen."

Angel knew how devastating a report would be to Valen. She was also afraid of what might happen if Eric Brannett ever learned of this. To Eric, she was money in the bank every year because of ticket and record sales. Valen had the great connections. Any threat to her, Valen's reputation or their relationship would hurt Eric's wallet!

"How much?" Angel asked.

"Ten thousand dollars, in cash. Monday morning."

Angel gave a vindictive sidelong glance. "Five thousand and you'll keep quiet."

"You're not in any position to bargain, Miss Frederick, and you know it."

She batted her eyelashes. "Fine, have it your way. Ten thousand dollars will be on your doorstep Monday morning."

Jesu tapped his driving hat, shut the limousine door, walked to the front of the automobile and got behind the wheel. Inching the partition down between them, he moved the back view mirror to see the woman sitting behind him. "Always a pleasure doing business with you."

Angel rolled the window back up, regretting the day she had ever met, Jesu A. Webb.

CHAPTER 20

The air surrounding Jono seemed to crackle with masculine charisma and vigor.

Never had Angel found a man so alluring. Like a statue of solid granite on top of a massive powerful beast, the man radiated authority and rugged, rustic beauty.

Every fine muscle on his brimming bare chest was glistening with sweat from the sweltering heat of the hot Colorado sun. His confident stature, his firm legs sporting chaps, his cowboy hat creating the aura of strength and virility of the American cowboy.

"Jono!" Angel screamed out of the limousine's window. Jono immediately rushed Wildshot down Counsel Hill toward the limousine which had stopped in the center of the road.

He dismounted as Angel leaped out of the limousine and into his large loving arms. Affectionately, he raised Angel high into the air, hugging and twirling her around in passionate, welcoming circles.

* * * *

They talked for hours that early morning, holding hands and sitting on top of Counsel Hill. They conversed of childhood dreams, past coincidences and lifelong wishes.

"I love spending time with you, Jono."

"I feel the same."

Together they watched Wildshot running below, across the golden grass fields, frolicking and flicking his long black tail at the colorful butterflies.

They admired his spirit and continued to enjoy the beauty of the land and nature surrounding them.

"Is this your favorite place to come and be alone?"

"Yes, how did you know?" he asked.

"Because if this was my ranch, I would come to this spot every day."

"This hill is very special to me. Something happened here that changed my life, Angel."

Jono began telling her of his first heroic deed, how he saved a baby mare from rolling down Counsel Hill after she had just been born. Angel didn't gloat over his endeavor, for she believed it was in Jono's nature to be so brave and caring. "I'm sure you've saved many other animals."

Jono told her another tale of his rescuing a calf from a vicious rabid dog. Finally, he said, "Not every woman would believe the things I'm telling you."

"I believe anything you tell me, Jono. You're my hero."

And the 'Cowboy' was, though he wasn't aware of it, playing the role of hero again. He was showing Angel what Jack himself had died trying to show her, what love was…

* * * *

"You look beautiful, Angel."

Her raven hair was blowing gently in the wind in wild disarray. The dress she wore was dainty and western styled. Just like he liked. She wasn't overly painted or wearing fancy flashy clothes. No, she looked just like an angel; Jono admired her as he stood and held out his hand.

"What is it, Jono?"

"Let's walk back to the house."

"Wonderful, I'd love to visit with your mother again."

"She's out today with some friends. She won't be returning until this evening."

Angel slowly rose, taking his hand. "Good, more time for us."

Jono began walking at an easy pace with Angel clutching his arm. They traveled down Counsel Hill into the fields of tall golden-green grass and prairie flowers, happily consumed with the wonder of being together.

"I've fallen in love with you, Angel."

She breathed in deeply the fresh air and picked a small sunflower by her feet as she passed. "My feelings for you, Jono, have grown as well."

He sat down onto a tree trunk with a smile. "I wish I could tell you how much." He patted the spot next to him for her to sit. "Friends shouldn't' keep secrets from one another, remember?"

"I just can't, Jono." She seated and gazed upward into the sun.

"The last time you were here you told me that you weren't afraid of Valen. Is it loving me that you're afraid of?"

"Yes."

"I would never hurt you, Angel."

"I know, but I'm not sure." She tried to turn away. He wrapped an arm around her.

"Tell me."

"I'm not afraid of Valen either. I'm just afraid of what would happen to you or Valen if the truth of how I feel were known."

Jono's hat shadowed his wondering expression. "Explain, Angel."

"I met Valen when I was still a teenager, after my parents died. He had heard of their deaths, and, I suppose, he felt sorry for me."

"Generosity is noble, Angel."

"Yes, well, I soon realized that Valen wasn't just noble; he needed my help. Valen was caught up in something pretty bad. Eric Brannett, a business partner of his, gave Valen some pills and now he is mixed up with drugs. So is my agent, Eric Brannett." Angel lowered her lashes. "Eric is the one that got Valen so addicted that now he can't seem to stop taking all these things."

"That must be very difficult for you."

"You have no idea. Valen can't seem to get off of them and I believe Eric wants Valen ill."

Jono took the sunflower out of her hand and laid it on the bark. "Isn't there a way?"

"Eric just keeps giving Valen new pills to hide the side effects of the other pills. He gets very sick, and his emotions are all over the place."

"I feel for him."

"Valen is good-hearted, but he lives constantly with guilt and pain. He can't always control his own actions. He even sometimes blacks out from the medications." Jono watched a cloud pass, giving her time to continue, and him to digest everything she'd shared.

"I honestly think the drugs are killing him, making him worse. I tell him, but he won't listen. He thinks the drugs are the only thing keeping him alive."

"You're keeping him alive." Jono smiled to her supportively. "Your love is."

"I wish I was strong enough to get him off those drugs and into a real good rehab program that can help him." Jono wrapped an arm around her.

"I feel like I should be doing more. I wish he would just listen to me. I wish my warnings meant more to him than taking those drugs."

"You sound angry."

"I am angry."

"At him?"

"No, at life." Angel's hands clutched together. "You see, Valen was an abused child. He learned early in life that by using drugs, he could forget that he was being beaten."

"How do you know he was beaten?"

"All you have to do is look at his hands." She swallowed hard. "They haunt me."

Angel fought to maintain her composure. "I guess that's why we understand each other. We've both been through so much. All Valen's ever wanted was to be loved and not have a family that won't turn away from us or abandon us. We both want that."

Jono pulled her to him. "I understand."

She wiped away a tear. "Do you?"

"Yes."

"I don't love him the way I love you." Angel opened her heart and forced the shell around it to come crashing down. "I love you like a lover and him more as a friend. But he's the one I owe for taking me in, giving me a career and loving me as a part of his family. He's all I've had for so long."

"I see."

"So many times, I've wanted to leave him. I've tried to make it work but every time I try to get close and personal with him, he backs away. He doesn't treat me as an equal."

"What if you were to back away?"

"I've tried to move on and then I saw what Eric Brannett was capable of."

Jono interrupted. "What happened?"

"After that, Valen's drug use increased."

"Whatever happens, Angel, don't regret growing close to me."

She gazed up into his big blue eyes. "And don't you ever regret that I love you."

"I wish you could be my wife instead of his."

Angel kissed his cheek, slowly breathing in his masculine scent. "I wish I would have met you before I met Valen."

"He needs you more than me right now, doesn't he?"

"I'm sorry, Jono."

He raised her head to his, causing their lips to be only centimeters apart. "Someday, we'll be together. Someday, you'll be my wife."

"How can you be so sure?"

"Love's a funny thing, Angel. If it's real, it never dies. Whether the person angers you or even moves away for years, it doesn't matter. Once you've found each other again, even if it's only for a moment, even if it's after death, the love is there. It doesn't matter how many arguments you get into or how long you're apart. Because when love is real, it lasts forever."

Angel stood in front of him, tears falling down her cheeks. "Then we will be together someday."

"Yes, we will. Have faith."

"It's like that verse, Jono, the one you told me. Love is patient; love is kind and will endure."

"Exactly." His mouth took hers, melting her clear to the core with unconstrained need and sad intoxication. For a moment, she forgot Valen and how much he needed her. She could only focus on her need, her need to kiss the only man she'd ever loved.

Being in his arms, she felt like an angel. Her heart seemed to sing. Her mind seemed to connect with its haven. She was able to touch the stars, earth and heaven.

"Well, isn't that sweet." The voice alerted them of an intruder.

Angel was released out of Jono's arms as he stood and faced Jesu.

The man was young, beautiful, a pretty man with a girlish face, blond shoulder-length hair, green dazzling eyes and a pug nose. He was wearing a black and white suit with a matching limousine driver's cap. A camera was in his hands.

"What do you want?"

"I've already taken everything I need." Jesu smiled. "Please, don't let me interrupt any further."

"You lying scumbag!" Angel screamed. "Give me the camera! You promised to keep Jono out of this!

"Aww," Jesu sarcastically sympathized. "Well, maybe my nose will grow along with my bank account."

"I wouldn't joke about such things," Jono warned. "Your fate has already been determined."

"What are you going to do, kill me? I see right through you! You're nothing but an overgrown sap! Love's funny, Angel… it's so kind… it's so patient." Jesu mocked him, brutally. "It can last for eternity."

Angel demanded. "Give me the camera!"

"Never," Jesu laughed. "Why the hell should I? Your cowboy doesn't have the guts to hurt a fly!"

CHAPTER 21

Jesu's hand reached for the limousine's door handle. Before his very eyes, the door locked. "What the…" Jesu backed away, then quickly dismissed the coincidence. "No, no I must have left it locked."

Carefully, he dug the key from out of a pant pocket, unlocked the door and slithered in behind the wheel of the limousine.

The cellular phone rang.

Across the passenger's seat, Jesu picked up the cellular phone receiver. "Hello, Jesu speaking."

"Have you determined your destiny yet?" Jesu slammed down the phone.

Ring! Ring! Ring!

Jesu became irritated and snatched the phone. "I sure know your destiny, Cowboy, a one-way ticket straight to hell once Eric Brannett gets through with you!"

"Jesu, is something wrong?"

Jesu straightened, realizing he was talking to Eric Brannett. "I'm sorry, Mr. Brannett. I thought you were someone else for a moment."

"Did you take any pictures of Angel and the kissing cowboy?"

"Yes, Sir."

"Good, when I receive the camera's memory card, you will receive my tape recording of your attempted blackmail."

Jesu took a belated breath. "I'll be at our destination in thirty minutes."

* * * *

Her dress was clinging to her frame. Her long raven hair was whipping in the wind as he started to chase after the beautiful woman running across the golden-green grass fields toward the limousine in the distance. "Angel, wait!"

"I can't!" she screamed back over her shoulder. "I have to catch Jesu before he shows those pictures to Valen!"

"Wait!" Jono easily matched her speed and then placed a hand on her shoulder to slow her down.

Angel stopped, gasping for air. Her face was flushed, and her body was shaking. "Jono, if Valen ever saw a picture of me kissing you, it could send Valen over the edge and I don't even want to think about what Eric Brannett might do. I have to follow Jesu! I have to stop him before it's too late!"

"Just wait a second." Jono lifted his large hands to his mouth and whistled three times consecutively.

Angel cried out, "I have no time for this!"

"Let me give you a ride."

"What ride?" When her gaze turned in Jono's direction, she saw Wildshot standing directly behind him.

"Come on," Jono mounted and held out his hand. "We'll catch him."

"A horse can't outrun a car."

"Wildshot can outrun any car." Jono smiled. "What's the matter? Don't you trust me?"

Angel placed her foot in the stirrup, took his hand and plopped herself down in front of him. "More than anyone."

"Yah!"

Angel grasped the saddle's horn as Wildshot jumped into a full-fledged run. "How fast?"

"Fast enough." Jono snapped the reins until Wildshot increased speed tenfold.

Dust, smoke and grass began to fly in a trail behind them. Angel couldn't comprehend the speed at which they were traveling. She gawked at the ground, whizzing past and turning from golden-green to one solid green blurb.

"Jono!" she shouted, afraid.

"Don't worry! Well catch up to your driver in time!" Angel had no doubt.

* * * *

Jesu beheld the dark and treacherous mountain road before him as the limousine climbed higher onto Mt. Brevity. The brick pavement was old, crumpling, beneath the weight of the heavy automobile. The metal side guardrails were rusted on every crooked twist and around every dangerous corner.

He reduced speed. "Jesu!"

Jesu heard his name being screamed through an open side window. "Jesu!"

Jesu glanced sideways to the outside rearview mirror and spotted the cause of the cry. "What the hell?" How could they possibly have been able to catch up to the limousine? "I'm not stopping for you, Bitch! I've got my own problems thanks to you."

He attempted to maneuver the limousine too quickly around a turn in the mountain's road.

Suddenly, Jesu lost control.

The back-half of the limousine fishtailed on the brick pavement and plummeted through a rusted side road railing.

"Aaaagh!"

Jesu slammed on the brakes, but his attempt to stop the limousine was useless. The unruly back half of the car pulled the limousine almost over the ledge, dangling, three hundred feet above the hard, Colorado ground.

Jono, witnessing the automobile falling, leaped off of Wildshot to the front of the limousine and grasped the bumper with all of his might.

Jesu couldn't breathe! He couldn't move, completely paralyzed with the fear of dying. He didn't dare look downward. He didn't dare take his foot off the brake.

"Open your door and jump to the ledge!" Jono dug his cowboy boots into the brick paved road and pulled with all of his might. "Jump!" The limousine was slowly falling. The elongated car seemed to be being yanked out of his grasp by some powerful force stronger than gravity.

Jesu glared at the cowboy trying to rescue him. His mouth was open wide as if trying to understand why any man would come to his aid, especially why this man would!

"Jump!" Jono was beginning to lose ground.

Jesu opened the door and leaped out onto the cliff's ledge. The moment his feet touched the surface, Jono released the automobile.

"Who? What are you?" Jesu asked.

The explosion of the car rocked Brevity Mountain. Jesu looked down, over the edge and watched the limousine burning in pieces. "You saved my life."

"I suppose I did."

"Didn't you realize that I'm carrying a camera's photo memory card that can destroy your relationship with Angel?"

"I am perfectly aware of that fact."

Jesu didn't comprehend. "Most men would have let me die."

"A selfish man would have."

Jesu pulled out the memory card from his camera which was lodged in his front pant pocket and handed it to Jono. "You really should learn that a man should look out for his own interests."

"I don't live that way."

Jesu began to turn away, up the mountain road. "You know, I could have kept that memory card. I was about to go up that mountain to my meeting destination with the man who wants to ruin your life. Now I am being blackmailed instead of you. You shouldn't have been so quick to save your enemy."

Jono crossed the road and stood feet away from him. "I don't believe anyone will think you survived that crash, do you? Wouldn't you rather appear dead, than alive to whomever you were supposed to show those photos to?"

Jesu's eyes flickered, intrigued with Jono's idea. "Maybe?"

"If everyone thought you were dead, you would be free to go and do as you please. You could even disappear."

"That sounds nice. Cowboy, you're forgetting one thing; there won't be any corpse for the forensic officers."

"I know the sheriff personally. He'll just run what's left of the tag, and believe me, as 'Luck' would have it, you're dead."

"You know the sheriff?"

"Let's just say, I know what's going to happen, and I'm willing to stake my reputation on it."

"What good is your reputation to me?" Jesu asked. "How do I know that's what going to happen? If the person I'm working for finds out I wasn't killed, believe me, I'd rather have been killed in that explosion."

"Trust me, I know."

"Why should I trust you?"

"Because I would never let harm come intentionally to anyone."

Jesu scratched his chin. "I can't believe I'm standing here, wasting my time, listening to you!"

"You're listening, because you'd rather have your death faked than continue to be indebted to Eric Brannett."

"You're right. He's blackmailing me with a recording. For all I know there could be a hundred copies." Jesu slowly extended his hand for Jono to shake. "How did you know?"

"Angel told me who she is really afraid of and who got Valen on drugs in the first place."

"I don't want to be indebted to you either for saving my life," Jesu said. Jono shook Jesu's hand.

"I just better appear dead, Cowboy."

"I'll see to it."

Jesu yanked his hand away and began to stroll downward toward the bottom of the mountain. "I don't know what, or who the hell you are, or how you even held up that limousine for so long; but whatever you are, I'm glad you saved my life."

Jono sighed, guessing that was the closest thing he'd receive as a thank you. "You're welcome."

Jesu quickly walked away.

"I never knew a man could be so brave," Angel uttered to Jono.

"God has blessed me with incredible strength," he said.

"With immeasurable courage." Angel cocked her chin, studying him. "And forgiveness."

"You didn't think I would try to save his life, did you?"

"I wasn't sure."

"Weren't you?"

"I wasn't sure if you could."

Jono grinned. "Never underestimate a Haze, Angel."

"You risked your life for someone who wasn't worth it."

"That's not for me to judge." Jono raised a brow. "A man can change his life."

"I'm not so sure," Angel pressed. "I think we should follow him and make sure he gave us the right memory card. He could have another one on his person."

"Go ahead, follow him, then."

"Won't you come with me?"

"No, I've got to go put out the flames before I go."

Angel immediately shouted, "That's suicidal!"

"Someone's got to put out those flames at the bottom of Brevity Mountain."

"We should hurry back to your ranch and call the fire department."

"If we go back to the ranch, there won't be a ranch by morning."

"Jono, you've already risked your life once today!" Angel grimaced. "We'll find a phone and call the fire department. Who do you think you are, the 'Cowboy'?"

Jono whistled and with a hand signaled Wildshot to transport Angel out of harm's way.

She got onto the horse's back and grasped the saddle's horn. As soon as Wildshot began to trot, Angel yelled, "Jono, stop this horse at once!"

"I'm sorry, Angel. I can't wait. Animals will die. Farms will be destroyed. I have to put out the flames now before they spread into town."

"That fire is too large for ten men to handle!" Wildshot carried her onward, down the mountain's twisting and turning road. "It's impossible for one!"

"You're underestimating me again, Angel."

"Jono, no!"

"I'm sorry." Jono jumped over the road's ledge and began climbing down the mountain, into the blazing inferno.

Angel turned to watch Jono's descent. "What man climbs fearlessly down into a wall of flames?" She leaped off of Wildshot's saddle and peered over the mountain's side.

Through the smoke, she watched him climb down the side of the mountain and hurry to the limousine. Once he had gotten as close as he possibly could, ducking the flames, he leaned over the grass surrounding the burning car and began pulling it out in hunks. With unbelievable speed, Jono dug a large circular ditch completely around the burning car to contain the fire.

Angel suddenly realized who Jono had to be, who Jono really was. What normal man could have done that so fearlessly and quickly? Jono wasn't just any cowboy. Jono was *the* Cowboy, the legend, himself.

"Cowboy!"

Jono heard his nickname being carried by the wind. He faced the direction of Angel's voice, calling from up above. She was leaning over the edge, staring down at him. "You *are* the Cowboy, aren't you?"

Jono admitted the truth by tapping his Cowboy hat and nodding.

Angel felt as if she had been a fool. How could she not have known? His horse ran faster than lightning. His strength was immeasurable. His heart was of gold and purely unselfish.

"Why didn't you just tell me?" With the fire completely contained, Jono whistled for his horse and Wildshot gave her a nudge from behind.

"Does he want me to ride down to him?" she asked the horse. Wildshot nickered thrice.

"That's a yes?" The enormous stallion repeated the nickering.

Angel assumed the answer. She placed her foot in the stirrup, grasped the saddle's horn and lifted herself into the saddle.

Once she was properly seated, Wildshot cantered down the mountain's brick paved road until he reached his master's side.

Several moments passed as Jono stroked Wildshot's mane.

Angel finally repeated the question, demanding an answer. "Why didn't you just tell me?"

Jono returned his hat to his head. His dirty face became half-shadowed by the sun, his chest glistened with perspiration. "I didn't think it should matter."

"You didn't think it should matter?"

"I thought you might start treating me different, like I'm some kind of freak, like everyone else does."

"Your family doesn't treat you like a freak." Angel swung herself out of the saddle and clutched one of his hands with her own. "And neither shall I."

Jono faced her, ashamed of not revealing all. "I'm sorry."

"Don't be." Angel's red lips curved into a smile. "There's been too many secrets kept between us."

"I wasn't sure if you'd understand."

"I know what it's like to be different."

"Do you, Angel?"

"As a singer in the limelight, people think all kinds of wrong stuff about me, whether it's true or not."

"At least you get respect when people look into your eyes; I see fear."

"Look into mine." She opened her eyes so wide she could see the reflection of her gray jewels dancing in his big blue pools. "Am I afraid of you?"

"No."

"I admire your courage. I admire everything you stand for."

"Because I'm the 'Cowboy'?"

"No." She laughed, heartily. "Because you're you and there's not too many around that love as you do."

"You admire me for that?"

"I more than admire you. I love you. From now on, Jono, let's have no more secrets between us."

"I think that's going to be an easy thing from now on, Angel, especially since you came here today to say good-bye."

CHAPTER 22

ngel was surprised that Jono had taken her to the airport. During the trip, he didn't say a word. He simply held her in his arms as Wildshot carried them to the back gate.

She didn't know what to say to him. She wanted to beg him to let her stay. Angel wanted to tell him she could stay forever. But she was perfectly aware that there were no words that could help their situation.

They could not be together as long as Valen was still in the picture, and she continued working with Eric Brannett.

The legend dismounted and slowly went to the back gate overlooking the small Madison airport. "Don't say goodbye, Angel, just go." He swung the gate open.

"You've accepted it. Haven't you?"

"That you might marry, Valen? No, I have not accepted it. I may have to live with it."

"I love you."

"I know." Jono watched her dismount and head through the metal gate. She was fighting her urge to cry.

"I think you're doing the right thing by marrying Valen and giving him the family he's always needed."

"We both finally find someone who we can talk to about everything and is equally as unselfish, and it's this unselfishness that is going to rip us apart. The truth is going to rip us apart."

Jono lowered his head and shut the gate between them. "Valen needs you until he can get his addiction to drugs under control."

Before he could take his hands away, Angel grasped the fence, encasing both his hands. "I feel like I'm never going to see you again."

Jono raised his head with the shadow from his hat now lifting above his eyes. Gazing in the blue depths, she felt as if she could see right into his soul.

"I don't want this, Jono. I want us to be together."

"What we want is irrelevant, Angel. Just go."

She understood Jono's pressing her to leave. Her debt to Valen and the people guarding her career over her happiness would always come between them.

"Please, not yet. Let's just stay here for a while." She gripped his hands tighter. "I feel like I'm never going to see you again."

"Sometimes you just have to trust. Sometimes you've just got to let go of the things that mean the most to you and hope they'll come back." Jono turned away. "Go home, Angel."

She watched him walk away from her, hoping to catch another glimpse of his beautiful, rugged face before she stepped onto the plane. But he never did turn around. He whistled for Wildshot, and Jono left as quickly as he had come.

CHAPTER 23

Before Angel stepped onto the plane, she went to a phone outside the airport's lobby and dialed Valen's number.

"Principessa, the phone in the limousine hasn't worked for hours. I've been trying to reach you."

"I'm fine." Angel replied. "I'm just about to get onto the jet back to New York."

"Excellent. When you return, be sure to stop by my estate. I need to inform you of the goings-on while you were away."

"Did something happen?"

"Your Colorado driver tried to blackmail me with a picture of you embracing a cowboy in front of a convenience store. He threatened to go to the press with it. I collapsed in Eric Brannett's office."

Angel knew then that she hadn't made a mistake by returning to Valen. "That must have been a picture of me with a fan. I believe he did give me a hug before I could stop him."

"Yes, that is what Brannett reminded me of. Now that you've done that country single and were on the cover of *Rock-N-Country Magazine* you willhave many fans in that area now. Eric Brannett fired Jesu and acquired the picture to keep it out of the press."

"Is that what Eric told you?" she asked. "Did you go to the hospital?"

"I'm fine. So did you enjoy your new driver?"

"He was great," Angel lied. "A matter of fact, since I'm coming to your estate anyway tonight, why don't you set me up a meeting with Eric so we can discuss it when I get back into town? I'd really like to give him a piece of my mind."

"I'll be sure to do that, Principessa, whatever you ask, is yours."

* * * *

She moved like a cat across the floor, dressed in a tight blue Victorian bodice, long flowing skirt, her angelic curls swirled into a French twist. Her smile was gleaming into the night. She embodied every man's desire—fire and innocence combined with enticing female elegance. And when she opened her apartment door, her beauty melted him to the core. Desire moved Valen forward, grasping, and kissing the top of her soft, alabaster hand.

"Hello, mio Principessa."

Valentino was a picture of courtly splendor. Royalty in black, he wore his tuxedo well. White satin gloves and a single white rose in his lapel adorned him dramatically. The color of the rose reflected in his dark brown eyes.

"Good evening, Valen."

Raising his head from over her hand, he gazed into her gray jewels. "How can any man be so lucky?"

She laughed.

Valen chivalrously took her petite arm and began escorting her. Proudly, he led her into the Royalty Complex's elevator, down six floors, and into the main hall. All eyes were on them, the couple who appeared as if they might have stepped right off of the red carpet, as they headed for the exit.

"You out did yourself tonight," Valen complimented, radiating his thoughts of her loveliness as she unconsciously swayed her slim hips with her white high heels clicking against the tile floor.

"Thank you."

Flashes began bombarding the couple as they maneuvered out into the night. The paparazzi yelled questions concerning their wedding scheduled for tomorrow. "Where is it?" They all wanted to know. "Where will the honeymoon be?"

The black limousine, shimmering in the darkness, was awaiting their arrival, the door being held by the driver. Angel swept past the cameras and, with a sensual cross of her long, luscious legs, lowered herself into the back. Valen followed with equal grace.

Fame, power, connections and money—how they seemed to be living the American dream. Every day, since Angel's return, she became more lost with it, drowning miserably within material goods and isolated from the man she loved.

"Would you care for a drink?" The limousine started and the cameras faded as Valen poured wine into a champagne glass.

"Yes."

He handed the glass to her.

As she sipped from her drink that sparkled in the moonlight, reminders lined the New York walkways. Beggars and prostitutes circled around the fire-lit trash cans to warm themselves from the night's cold air. She had once been on the street, a runaway, after her parents' deaths.

It was Valen who had helped her.

"No man will be paying attention to the speaker tonight, Principessa. One deep breath and your lovelies will be poking out to say hello."

Angel awoke from her daydream, not knowing what he had just said. "Pardon?"

Valen took her hand. "Normally, remember that I do not approve of such low-cut... well, in public." His eyes barely wandered there. "Tonight, though, let the men gawk at what will soon be mine, my fortune, my most priceless fortune, my wife."

Her eyes drifted back to the people on the streets until the Great Opera House came into view. More paparazzi swarmed the limousine as it stopped in front of the all-star Opera House.

The limousine door was soon opened by the doorman and Angel exited onto the red carpet and into the line of fire.

"When's the wedding," journalists shouted, pushing one another for better pictures and sticking their microphones higher in the couple's faces.

Valen wrapped a protective arm about Angel and hurried her through the annoyance with ease, until they were inside the benefit show of the Great Opera House.

All eyes were on them as they entered the building, taking the quickest way up the stairs to the highest balcony, avoiding the black-and-white decked-out crowd. They strolled up each step, her blue dress train cascading down behind.

When they reached the balcony, he pushed away the red curtain, ushering her inside. "I love you," he uttered as she passed him. "You're the only happiness I've ever known."

Angel felt her heart breaking.

Valen had been nothing but kind, thoughtful and generous since her return from Colorado. Never before had he been so attentive or easy going! Their upcoming wedding had mellowed him to the core.

Even still, she missed the man she truly loved.

They seated themselves in two of the four seats in the darkest corner of the balcony and were enjoying the peace until another couple entered.

"Angel, a man in the galley told us you two were up here. Love the dress; it's from the Girranti collection, isn't it? It's just to die for this fall."

Valen rolled his eyes heavenward as the couple seated themselves next to them. The woman was a tall, blonde bombshell, Shari, a Marilyn Monroe look-alike, who was in the process of trying to wrangle a singing contract with Eric Brannett as her agent. Tonight, she was on the arm of one of her actor friends, Brad Pitelli.

"Yes, I love yours as well." Angel lied, but it was their normal lack of meaningful conversation.

"So when are we going to set me up for rehearsal with that song writer of yours? I would love to show you how I can sing, Angel."

"Call Eric Brannett's office, and he'll set something up for you."

Suddenly the spotlights shifted on the stage and a speaker entered the room.

"Good evening." The speaker was wearing a flowered bow tie with matching trousers; obviously, he was some kind of comedian. "Tonight's benefit is not a laughing matter. The Opera House has opened its doors for a fantastic organization."

Valen leaned over and decreed in her ear, "I'm giving this benefit ten thousand tonight."

"That's wonderful." Angel wasn't sure which benefit show he had taken her to tonight.

"Yes, I believe it is a good cause."

In her soul, Angel knew exactly whom she loved and wanted to marry. Deep down, she knew it wasn't the man sitting next to her, but Jono. Her heart belonged to Jono, her beloved cowboy. But how could she not stay, when Valen had done so much for her, when he needed her.

Even with all Valen's problems with Eric, Jack's murder, and his overbearing ways, Valen was the very reason she was still alive. He was the one who took her off the streets, gave her a career, fame, fortune, everything and anything she ever wanted in material possessions. All he'd ever asked for in return was that she remain with him and be someone he could depend on.

She had already failed his trust with Jono. How could she, in good conscience, abandon him now? Valen, though he was cold because of his wicked past, didn't know how to relate to anyone differently. The only skills he learned growing up were results of pain, violence, control and constant drug abuse.

Suddenly, claps awoke Angel, and she began to clap along as a young, Asian-American man rolled across the stage in a wheelchair.

Angel could feel the tears coming, missing Mrs. Haze as well. How she loved her. Every part of her smile, the way her eyes lit up when she saw Angel. Mrs. Haze made her feel so completely loved, not as a possession, but for who she was. Yes, for who she was, not even that she sang or what kind of designer clothes she might have on that day.

Ever since she was a child that was all Angel had ever heard. "Isn't she beautiful? Isn't she growing up to become a man killer? Oh, and what a voice!"

Now she was about to become an ornamental wife with Jack's murder caused by her previous actions. It was all she could do to not to get another man killed or Valen himself.

CHAPTER 24

Jono was riding like lightning atop Wildshot, through twisting tumbleweeds, stampeding cattle and thrashing rain, to warn his brother of the howling tornado which had suddenly fallen from out of the Colorado sky.

It was the largest twister Jono had ever seen. An onslaught of rocks and dust tore rapidly across the land, rendering everything in its path barren, devastating God's creation, engulfing life, feeding then spitting death out in return.

No matter how hard he pressed through swirling wind, flying sticks and tree branches, the tornado surpassed Wildshot in less than a minute and was engulfing LaFordge's land.

"Please, God, don't let anything happen to my brother!"

The twister continued to recede into the darkness beyond with a distant roar. All that remained in view of the awesome storm was the lightning strikes that lit up the sky and the pounding rain that beat against Jono's bare chest.

Through a quarter mile of broken trees and ravaged land, Jono made his way onto the front of LaFordge's property. The destruction was minimal, considering. LaFordge's two-story house was hardly touched; only the screens and windows were blown out. But the stable was crushed, strewn around beyond any repair or recognition. Wood was scattered as far as the eye could see, along with one dead horse, a dog and two heifers. It was a miracle the damage wasn't worse.

A faint noise being carried by the wind alerted Jono of someone in need of assistance. He ordered Wildshot immediately around the house to assess where the whimpers were coming from.

Then he saw them.

His two brothers were crouched, trying to lift a large gray rock about twenty feet away from the house. A woman was underneath. Jono dismounted and hurried toward them.

"It's Martha!" Bear announced.

The rock covered one leg, one arm, and a part of Martha's chest. Her breathing was shallow; her face was as pale as a ghost's.

Jono quickly took charge. "Don't worry, Martha, we'll get the rock up! Just try to crawl out as soon as we lift high enough!"

"Okay."

Snatching the rock by its deep crevices in the sides, Jono wrapped his massive arms around the middle of the rock. Bear was to his right. LaFordge was grasping the rock to his left. Together they began lifting.

The rock seemed heavier to Jono than anything he had ever raised. He was too emotional to clear his thoughts and concentrate. The sight of his youngest sister like this, a woman so beautiful and strong, crushed like nothing, cut into his soul, making him weak, eliminating his strength by half.

Then he heard a loud "Snap!"

Jono's shoulder suddenly dislocated, and the rock began to fall down toward the ground. The brothers struggled, gripping, groaning, to save her. They screamed out, "No," but their attempts were useless. The rock tumbled to the earth.

Jono's eyes closed as tight as they could. He couldn't bear to witness the death of his sister, his sweet sister. His left arm was completely numb and his heart was thumping out of his chest. He couldn't look! He couldn't breathe! "I killed her!"

Bear wrapped an arm around Jono's trembling back. "Don't say that! It wasn't as much your fault as mine."

LaFordge was still gripping the rock trying to lift it. He would not give up, even now.

Jono cried out, "Stop. She's dead, LaFordge!"

Bear pulled LaFordge away from the rock. LaFordge bolted around, tightened his fist, and swung at Bear.

The punch missed.

"She's not dead!" LaFordge roared. "She's not dead. Martha's not dead."

Jono heard a faint cry over the noise of his two brothers arguing. He immediately raised his hat and listened for the words again.

"Stop it. Stop it, you two." Jono assessed where the voice was coming from and glanced around the rock to find her.

Martha's foot was barely an inch away from the rock's edge but somehow, she had been able to roll out from underneath in such a short amount of time.

"Um, Boys!" Jono called. They were still fighting, screaming at one another, blaming each other for Martha's death.

"Bear, LaFordge!"

Bear screamed at him. "What?"

"She's not dead."

LaFordge and Bear ran to his side and fell to their knees down beside her. Her sandy blonde hair was covered with dirt. Her brown eyes were barely open. But she was breathing, alive.

"I'll go get the medicine man!" LaFordge ran toward his stallion.

"Get Whitefeather, too!" Jono pleaded. LaFordge glared over his shoulder and raced away without a word.

"He won't get Whitefeather," Bear reminded Jono as he reached down to hold Martha's hand. "He doesn't believe in modern medicine."

"Then I'll get him."

Bear examined Jono's bare shoulder. Once where the broad line was sleek and smooth, a bump now rose in the center of the blade. He shoulder was broken. "You need him, too."

"I'll fetch him, and he'll work on both of us." Jono's white smile brightened.

"Help me sit!" Martha suddenly screamed.

"You should rest," Jono said.

"Help me sit!" Martha ordered.

Jono aided her with his good arm until Martha sat upright. "You need to know something."

Jono instantly sensed the seriousness of what Martha was about to say. "What is it?"

"Go home, Jono, take Bear."

"I've got to find Whitefeather."

"LaFordge will find a doctor for me." Martha's expression turned ghastly bleaker. "There's a twister heading south. The winds will push it west, right onto the ranch. Look!"

Jono and Bear took one glance and in a few quick strides jumped onto the backs of their horses. They needed to return to the Haze ranch as quickly as they possibly could. Jono's land was in the path of a tornado, and so was their grandmother.

Six hours later, 4:00 a.m.

CHAPTER 25

The smell of death rotted his senses as LaFordge went to the fallen chair in the back of what was left of Jono's barn. The wooden walls still stood except for the four holes that had been made by flying animals bursting through them from the tornado's wild winds. Dead animals, several chickens, a cowbird and a deer lay sprawled in pieces as he made his way through the bloody mess.

It was late in the night as he upturned the chair and seated himself. Slowly, his head tilted up to gaze at the roof. Instead of a roof, he found brilliant stars beaming down at him. It all seemed so distant, so strange to witness such starry beauty and at the same time be aware of how every minute in life is precious.

LaFordge covered his face with his hands. His heart was weighing heavily, remembering his grandmother's motionless body.

Quietly, he began to weep.

All alone, he shed his tears, for that was the only way that LaForge would.

* * * *

Angel was restless. She was dreading the wedding scheduled for a few hours away and decided to take a late-night stroll in her complex's garden.

It was a beautiful night. The stars were shining as she walked around the white Greek statues and gazed over the garden flowers. She admired the roses and violets, walking slowly, thinking about how her life had changed over the past year.

She missed Jono.

Out of the corner of her eye she caught a glimpse of a man standing beside a large water fountain in front of her.

He was wearing a long black trench coat and a black cowboy hat that seemed to cover over half his face.

Angel held her breath. Who would be out at this time of night? She turned around and was about to walk away.

"Angel."

The western drawl sounded familiar.

She pivoted and a handsome man came out from the shadows. His rugged features were covered with dirt and scraps. His clothes were filthy and soaking wet.

"Bear? Aren't you Jono's brother?" He didn't return the smile with which she greeted him. Instead, he moved forward, standing directly in front of her.

"I'm sorry to bother you at this time of night. I got on a plane as quickly as I could to make sure someone from my family told you in person." He sighed, heavily. "A tornado went through Madison."

Angel's heart skipped a beat. Her chemise dress fell off a shoulder as she inquired in horror, "Is Jono all right?"

"No. None of us are."

Angel gasped in desperation. "He's not dead!"

"No, but our grandmother was in her bedroom when a part of the second story pancaked down on top of her."

"Nooo!"

"Jono tore up every board covering her, but he was too late." Her sudden sob caused him to drop his voice to nearly a whisper. "I wanted you to know. She thought of you like a daughter."

"Damn it, why?" Bear moved closer to her.

"I'm so sorry, Bear. I'm so sorry for your whole family and all her friends."

He looked into her teary eyes and pulled her to him, taking her shuddering frame into his masculine arms. She was his brother's woman. He felt an obligation to be there for her, to treat her as if she was part of the family.

Angel gazed up into his eyes which were almost as blue as Jono's. "I can't even tell you how much I'm going to miss her."

"I know."

"Is there anything I can do for your family?"

"Come back with me. My brother needs you."

"I wish I could, but I can't."

"Because of your wedding? I need to say something and I don't think I'm stepping out of bounds. I know how my brother feels about you. Every time you two look at one another, the world seems to disappear. I know you're not in love with the man you're supposed to marry. Come back with me, now, before you make the biggest mistake of your life."

"You don't understand."

"I understand how much my brother treasures you. Right now, you may be the only person who can pull him out of this. He's never lost anyone before. He's too used to being everybody's hero."

Angel was overcome with strong, conflicting emotions. The wedding was mere hours away, the man she loved too many miles away. She didn't want to marry Valen, not today, not ever.

The fear was paralyzing—fear of leaving Valen, fear of what the pain would do to him.

But Jono needed her now, more than even Valen did this time. Jono's life was burning up around him, swallowing him up with grief and sorrow. She knew it, like she knew it in herself, how devastating a death of a close family member could be.

"I just can't go back with you."

Bear slowly bent down and kissed her cheek. "Don't do this, don't make this mistake. You'll regret it for the rest of your life. Just follow me. Follow me home to Madison. Follow your heart."

He released her and began walking away. His black trench coat rippled in the wind. His long blond hair flowed out from beneath his black hat. He was a virile man, full of mystery, like his brothers.

"Why should I?" Angel asked. "I can't bring her back. I can't marry Jono."

Without turning toward her, he answered, "Jono deserves the same happiness as Valen."

"I want to be there for him. I just can't."

"That is your choice."

She was blinded by her loyalties to Valen. "I have no choice."

She sniffled in ragged breaths. She knew exactly what she wanted to do the moment Bear told her of the tragedy. She wanted to fly back into Jono's arms and hold him. Somehow they would find the courage together to go on and make some sense of this.

The wedding would have to wait, even if it meant lying to Valen about the reasons why she was going, so he wouldn't question her motives or worry.

Bear continued on without glancing back to her. This time she followed. He heard her high heels clicking behind him, and he smiled as only a Haze could, brilliantly.

CHAPTER 26

When Angel had come to him in the middle of the night ranting and raving about Mrs. Haze and a tornado, Valen immediately forbade her the use of his private jet. However, he should have known Angel wouldn't take no for an answer.

She was too worried that Mrs. Haze wasn't all right. "Bloody hell!"

Valen sank down onto her couch. "I should have given her permission to leave." At least then, he could have kept an eye on her and made sure she returned in time for their wedding.

Now, not only would they have to postpone their wedding, but he'd also have to reserve a commercial flight out of New York to Madison instead of using his own plane. Angel had stolen his private jet.

Valen reached across the coffee table for the phone when he noticed Angel's television had been left on.

"Around the clock, firefighters, E.M.T's, police and ambulance workers are continuing to dig men, women and children out of the rubble in Madison, Colorado. Here is Ken MacDowell with a live report."

Valen watched a reporter in his late twenties appear on the screen. He was clutching a gray microphone tightly in one hand and approaching a woman to be interviewed.

"Nikky, can you make a statement on behalf of your family at this tragic time?"

"Yes," the woman stepped forward, "I would like the public to know that the grandmother of the 'Cowboy' has passed away."

"What happened?"

"The tornado ripped down half of our family ranch when my grandmother was still inside."

Valen was fascinated. The woman was beautiful. She had reddish-brown hair, brown eyes and the carriage of royalty. The woman reminded him of someone, but who?

"Was the 'Cowboy' unable to help?"

"My brother was miles away at the time."

"Grace Haze was a well-loved woman in this small farming community. My heartfelt apologies for your family's loss, Nikki."

"Thank you."

Valen rose, remembering exactly who the woman reminded him of—the cowboy Angel had been holding in the picture Jesu had given him. The woman looked like him and Grace Haze.

Mrs. Haze was his grandmother! A grandmother that he lived with! Angel hadn't been alone when she visited Mrs. Haze! Mrs. Haze lived with the cowboy who had his arms all over Angel, touching and embracing her in that picture!

"Bloody hell!" Valen couldn't even think straight. He picked up the telephone and threw it across the room.

"She's been lying to me. She's been visiting not only Mrs. Haze but her grandson as well. She's been with that cowboy all this time. She's even spent the night there."

Could Angel be sleeping with another man? He'd allowed her to be in Madison! He'd been such a fool believing that she loved him!

* * * *

Rain beat against her skin as Angel climbed out of the rent-a-car remembering what had brought her here so many months ago.

Her car accident!

How her life was changed: Sometimes for the better, sometimes for the worse, but her life had drastically changed since. Never had Angel imagined she would care so much for that dirty cowboy that pulled her out of the wreckage.

At first, she didn't even like him. But with his undying charm, he'd grown on her. Maybe it was the way he always smiled at her or laughed at even the jokes she told which weren't really funny. Perhaps it was the simple way he listened to everything she said, or how wonderful he felt in her arms; that was why she fell in love. Whenever or however didn't matter though, only that she had fallen in love with him.

Through the wind and rain, she saw a glimpse of Jono in the grass field behind what was left standing of the devastated house. He was on his knees. She could see his hat clearly over the tall grass. His shoulders were trembling as he rocked back and forth.

No matter what the circumstances returning to New York would cause in the future, she was glad she had come back to Madison. Jono needed her. Angel began to run across the golden-green field toward him. The wet grass and dirt were beneath her feet. As rain drizzled down her face and arms, she wondered just what she could say that might ease his grief.

She halted a few feet behind him when she saw how his enormous body uncharacteristically looked so vulnerable.

Her heart quickened, so did her breathing. It was all she could do to not cry with him. For now, she knew she must be strong. Jono needed a friend, someone to lean on, talk to, to be a rock as solid as he once was.

At his knees before him was his grandmother's grave, recently dug, the topsoil turning to mud with the constant returning showers. There was no marker. Grace Haze's grave was a simple pile of fresh, dug earth.

Angel circled around to look Jono straight in the eyes. She wanted to greet him like she had dreamed of since the day she had left. But she didn't like seeing the evidence of his pain. His eyes were red and so swollen that only tiny slits were open. His face seemed to have aged since the last time she'd seen him, and he was pale, too pale. In his shaky hands, Jono was clutching a grave marker, a large wooden cross with "Grace" carved deeply into one side.

Her heart broke, once, twice, three times until she got her emotions back under control. She steeled herself to what she was feeling, hiding how Mrs. Haze's death had affected her. Truthfully, she could have easily fallen down beside him and wept right along, for she too had lost ones she'd loved.

Angel sank to her knees and noticed his breathing becoming more prominent. Even though Jono wasn't acknowledging her, he knew she was there. Angel was sure of it—just as sure as she was about how very miserable she had been without him.

"Jono." Her voice trembled in the rain as she fought to keep her emotions under control. Her voice sounded like an angel's to him.

"Everything's going to be all right." And her hand touched his shoulder. Brushing over a bump that rose in the center of a massive limb, she realized when he flinched that his shoulder was either broken or dislocated.

"Bear told me that you haven't slept. Will you come inside with me? I brought you some food and water."

His head lowered. His swollen eyes never left the grave. He looked as if he wished to crawl beneath the dirt and be with his grandmother.

"Please, Jono, come with me. I love you." She hoped her admission would gain his attention. It didn't. His large, calloused hands only tightened around the single wooden cross, as big tears dropped from his eyes, mixing with the rain that had soaked through his hat and skin.

She prayed quietly for the strength to take the cross and place it where it was meant to be, to bring some finality to his grandmother's death.

She raised a shivering hand to take the cross marker.

"No!" his deep voice bellowed, his grasp only tightening around Christ's symbol.

Her hand fell down to her side as tears did come into her eyes. This was going to be harder than she had anticipated. Jono was destroyed; there seemed to be no more light in his blue eyes, no spark that flickered even from her being there.

"Please, come back with me into the house. Part of the bottom floor is still dry."

"I can't. Not back into that house!"

She understood not wanting to go back where his grandmother had died, to what had caused it. She desperately wanted to hold him. He looked so lost, hurt and cold. This was a pain that neither he nor she would ever be able to forget.

"I should have built a stronger house."

Angel snapped up and shook him roughly by the waist. "Stop it!" Their eyes locked into a battle. "This isn't your fault! It's not the house's fault! It was her time to go."

"Not her! Why her? Why?"

Angel recognized that she had felt the same way hours ago. "I don't know. Only God can answer that."

She suddenly gained courage with his eyes on her, and her hand moved around the cross. Slowly, inch by inch, she lifted it out of his hand while she watched his pain move throughout his body in waves of heart-wrenching emotion.

"I'm sorry, Jono. I wish I could bring her back!"

Jono's head fell to the muddy dirt. He couldn't watch as the cross flew up then plummeted down, marking the grave.

"Come with me into the house. We can't live out in this kind of weather. Please, it's so cold."

"I can't."

Angel crawled through the wet dirt and grass to his side and wrapped her tender arms around his neck, pulling him forward next to her body. She wanted to prove how much she cared. "Jono, no matter how long you wait here, she's not here anymore; she's in heaven."

His head lifted and rested upon her lap. "I know," was all he said.

* * * *

Martha was leaning heavily against the back wall of the barn. Every second it seemed harder and harder for her to stand. The pain in her ribs constricted her breathing, the aching in her leg throbbed wickedly and more and more she was becoming faint.

In the distance, she heard the scuffle of footsteps coming toward her and she straightened up as much as possible. She could not let whoever was approaching witness her like this, so weak.

"So, where's Wildshot?" She watched LaFordge's large shadow dance across the barn wall in front of her.

"Meryl couldn't find him," LaFordge answered, staring at his sister's back. "The stallion must have run off."

"Meryl just didn't know where to look." Suddenly the wall before her eyes spun rapidly and she swayed slightly on her feet until she closed her eyes. She then got the shaky illusion under control.

LaForge moved up behind her. "You've been out here too long. Maybe you should come to my ranch and rest. Jono's girlfriend is here now."

"Nonsense, I'm fine."

"I see the rock broke your brain as well," LaFordge scoffed.

She slighted him a sidelong calculating glance. "I said, I feel fine." And she swung around on her unbroken leg to face him and prove it.

His brown eyes were on her like a hawk, waiting to catch her if she should fall or pass out form the pain. Martha looked exhausted and in agony, but he knew as long as there was any strength left in her, she would stay to aid Jono.

"Did Meryl check the corral?"

"Yes, she checked all the normal places Wildshot goes when Jono jumps off. She's still checking Counsel Hill."

"And Meryl is giving the whistle?"

"Yes, Wildshot must be ignoring her call."

Her features mixed into a subtle frown. "That doesn't make sense."

"I'm only telling you what Meryl said."

"Well, she's wrong!" Martha immediately regretted raising her voice by the sharp pains that crushed her breath. "I guess I'll have to find Wildshot myself. Tell Bear to saddle up Sunfire and I'll find him."

LaFordge stiffened into a worried stance. "You can't get on a horse, let alone ride one right now! The only place you're going is to bed!"

"Wildshot is out there, and Jono needs him!" The barn was growing darker to Martha. The light was fading in and out. "And I'm fine."

"Wildshot can take care of himself; he happens to not be as stubborn as my sister."

"Stubborn, are you saying that I'm stubborn? Saying I'm not fine?"

"And I suppose all those bandages you're sportin' are just my imagination, the leg's fine, the arm, the ribs, all that is fine."

Martha knew her womanly pride was losing out to brotherly concern. "Now, you're going to go straight to bed."

"I will when I'm good and ready; right now, I'm finding Wildshot. Jono's having a hard enough time dealing with all this without knowing Wildshot is missing!"

"You're hurt, remember?"

"Do I look hurt to you?"

He made no comment. "I'll find Wildshot, if you'll go home to bed, Martha."

She was shaking her head to clear away the cob-webs and dull the ring in her ears more than she was to argue. "I'll go."

LaFordge took a few steps forward and wrapped his arms around her slim waist. "Nikky will be coming back to the ranch after she talks to the reporters, and you shouldn't be here when she returns."

The weight leaning on him was growing more and more heavy.

"No, someone's got to find Wildshot. What if something happened to Jono's horse?"

Martha fell completely forward, losing all consciousness, submitting to the pain and fatigue. LaFordge held on for dear life until he had lowered her to the ground as softly as he possibly could.

He sighed as he released her and swiped her blonde hair from out of her face. "You stubborn woman! One of these days I'm going to tell Jono how loyal you are to him."

CHAPTER 27

Angel opened her purse and lifted a small Bible that she had purchased at the airport. She wrapped an arm around Jono and began to read, "I am the resurrection, and I am life. Those who believe in me, even though they die, yet shall they live, and whoever lives and believes in me shall never die. I am Alpha and Omega, the beginning and the end, the first and the last. I died, and behold I am alive forevermore, and I hold the keys of hell and death. Because I live, you shall live also."

After she had read the verses, she gazed at Jono. His head was raising, and his hat was in his hands over his heart. "Is there a verse you would like me to read?"

"Psalm 56:13."

"For thou has delivered my soul from death, yea, my feet from falling, that I may walk before God in the light of life."

"Read it again."

"For thou has delivered my soul from death, yea, my feet from falling, that I may walk… that I may walk… before God in the light of life." Angel fluttered her raven lashes, fighting her tears.

"That was my grandmother's favorite verse because she knew that someday she'd be able to walk again."

"It's wonderful."

Jono noticed her trembling. "You're frightened of the storm."

Angel smiled. "Yes, but I'm more worried about you right now." "You're shaking."

"I'm just upset." "And cold."

Jono took a deep breath and rose. "You shouldn't be out here; you should be inside."

"I'm not going anywhere without you."

Slowly, reluctantly, he took her hand and began leading her away from the gravesite toward the house. "I'm not going in, but I'll walk you to the porch to make sure you're okay."

"Thank you."

Nothing was left of the Haze's gardens but dirt and pulled up weeds. The sunflowers and vegetable plants had been demolished. Instead, wooden boards and furniture raked across the earth in pieces, scattered and broken as far as the human eye could see, littering the range into a wasteland. The barn was now useless. Horses and cattle were roaming free. The only structure that remained almost untouched was the house's front porch, and even there, screens had been ripped apart and tossed every which way. This home once filled with such life, memories and love now only stood as one giant catastrophe where dreams had literally blown away in seconds with the simple twist of the wind.

"I don't want to go any further." They had traveled as far as the first step inside the porch when Jono suddenly turned around, unwilling to witness the damage inside the house where his grandmother had been killed.

"At least we're out of the rain. Just wait right here and I'll find something for you to change into." She hurried into the living room, maneuvering around fallen wooden debris and wet puddles to the closet closest to the stairs. She wanted to find anything that Jono could warm himself with.

On one hanger was a pair of blue jeans and a dress white button-down shirt. There was a towel lying on the kitchen table; she snatched them all and crossed cautiously back, ducking underneath beams to the porch where Jono waited.

He was sitting next to one of the porch's posts, leaning against it. Her heart went out to him. "I found some clothes for you."

"You're the one trembling, Angel. Maybe you should put them on." She kneeled down beside his enormous frame and began wiping the rain beads from off his bare chest with a towel.

His swollen blue eyes turned to hers for an instant. In his gaze was a hint of acceptance; then he took the towel and jeans out of her hands. "I guess you're more worried about me than yourself," Jono said.

"I love you," she whispered.

Jono simply rose and said, "Turn around and I'll change."

After the rustle of clothes falling and the swoosh of dry ones being put on, he announced matter-of-factly: "I'm done."

Angel pivoted.

The clean clothes couldn't camouflage the desperation in his stance or the shallowness of his breathing.

"Is there anything I can do to help?"

"Be my wife instead of Valen's," he said.

"Jono, please! Don't you think that we've got enough to deal with, without discussing our relationship?" Angel walked away toward the rent-a-car to retrieve the food she had bought for him.

She needed time. She didn't want to be reminded of the fatality of their attraction when she was having a hard enough time accepting Mrs. Haze's death.

Several minutes had passed. When she returned, Jono was drying his short hair with the towel. "You shouldn't have come here, Angel."

Angel placed the bag on the floor in front of him. "I'm sorry you feel that way. I thought you would want me to come."

"Of course, I wanted you to come." Jono cocked a brow. "But you've got other responsibilities that take priority."

"Right now, I don't care about Valen—only you," she pressed. "You need me and that's all that matters. I want to be here for you as long as I can."

"That's just it, Angel. You can only stay as long as you can."

The bitterness in his voice surprised her. "Jono, do you think I want to ever leave you?"

"I know how you feel."

"Have your feelings for me changed?"

"Love lasts forever, Angel."

She breathed in those words as if they were the very oxygen that kept her alive. "That's right, Jono. And as long as we're together, we can survive anything."

"You have to leave. You're coming back here only reminds me. I'm fed. I'm warm. You did your friendship duty. Now get off my land."

"What?"

"Go back to Valen."

Angel jumped as if he had shouted those words to her. "You can't be serious! You need me now! I need you, now!"

"At what cost?" He saw the confusion on her face, and it hardened his resolve. "Get off my land, Angel. You're doing more harm than good for me and Valen."

CHAPTER 28

Her heart strings unraveled as she headed toward the porch doorway. Jono reached out and whirled her around, closing the gap between them.

His lips plunged down and captured hers with hard, unbridled passion.

Even though her lips were cold from the drizzling rain they soon melted under his fiery touch. She was being mesmerized by his intoxicating kiss and the burning emotions that the kiss was bringing, racing through her veins.

"Do you still want to leave?" Jono questioned heavily against her lips.

"No."

He released her and grabbed the towel across the porch. He held it out to her. "Dry off. This shirt is big enough for you to wear as a dress."

"My staying won't upset you, then?" Angel took the towel and began wiping off her arms.

"I don't want you to go, not really. I never did."

For the first time since his grandmother's death, Jono smiled. She had thought that he would never be able to smile again. She hardly could remember when to breathe, let alone strive for happiness. But now, gazing up into the love radiating down from his eyes just for her, Angel couldn't help wondering. God willing, they may still become man and wife.

Angel glanced back to the destruction inside the house. "I hope you're going to rebuild our house."

"Our house." His eyes brightened with her use of the term, "our house".

"Your grandmother would have wanted you to rebuild."

He nodded in agreement. "Yes, she would. I just don't believe it will be the same without her."

"No." Angel's black eyelashes fluttered. "It will still be okay, though, you'll see."

He pulled her back into his arms. "It will be more than okay if you'll give me the honor someday of being your husband."

"Yes, someday."

"Angel, I'm known for doing the impossible."

"Yes, that's true." Angel raised her chin to gaze into his beautiful big, blue eyes. "Rumor has it you're some kind of hero."

Her thin hands reached up and touched the well-defined muscles on his naked suntanned chest, surrendering to her innermost desires.

"Tell me, Angel." He enjoyed the feel of her hands rubbing against his chest. "Did you explain to Valen why you had to miss your wedding?"

"Not about everything."

Angel's head was lowering, their lips only inches apart. "Then let's hope he doesn't try to find you."

"I explained as well as I could, considering." He sighed against her lips. Her hands moved slowly upward until they encircled his thick muscular neck, his hair entangling in her fingernails.

"I hope you didn't endanger his health."

She gasped as he slightly pulled away, making her yearn for further closeness. "Everything will be fine. I should even be able to stay another couple of hours without any problem."

"Good, then whenever you're ready, we'll start rebuilding our house."

"Me?" The words exploded against his lips. "Do I look like a woman who knows anything about building a house?"

He chuckled against her lips. "You look like a lady smart enough to learn how."

"Yes, I bet I could, high heels and all, and outdo you in the process." They laughed close to each other's lips.

"I love your spunk, Angel."

"And I love your smile."

She kissed his lips, freeing the want and desire that was tearing her apart. Lord, he was amazing! The feel of his skin was magical. The taste of him was wine. Even her knees went weak as his tongue entered between her lips.

She pulled away slightly. "Is something wrong?"

"I don't know." Suddenly he moved around her, staring out across the barren, devastated land.

"Jono, what is it?"

"Put on the dry clothes." He started heading out of the porch, grabbing his cowboy hat. "I think someone's coming."

"Where are you going?" she called after him as another clash of thunder rocked her ears.

"To the field, to whistle for Wildshot. If he's around, he'll help me search the ranch. You look so beautiful, but I have to leave." Jono glanced over his shoulder. "I'll be right back."

Angel began drying off with the towel again, and then began putting on the dry white button-down shirt Jono had left for her. Just as she finished clasping the last button on the shirt, she heard a roar.

Slowly, she faced the noise. Coming toward the house, a long, sleek, black limousine was headed down the dirt path.

Valen had returned to Madison.

CHAPTER 29

Valen was a vision, as handsome as a man could be, model-perfect in his navy lapel jacket. His healthy midnight hair was stylish and pulled back into a tight Viking ponytail—his normal fashion. His body was sleek with masculine grace as he opened the limousine door and stepped out into the mud.

He acknowledged her with a nod.

Angel stumbled toward him like a frightened mouse trapped by an unpredictable cat. He lifted her chin with one gloved finger, forcing her gaze into his troubled brown eyes. "Where is he?"

"Where is who?" She plucked her chin out of his hand and glanced to the ground, avoiding his haughty glare.

"You're standing, half-naked in a man's shirt, Principessa. I believe that deserves some sort of explanation on who the owner is!"

"This shirt I found in Mrs. Haze's room after I came in from the rain. It must be her ex-husband's."

Valen quickly moved away from her, toward the porch. "Valen, where are you going?"

"I'm going into the house to search."

Angel quickly stepped in front of him, blocking his path. "Search for who? No one else is here."

"Pity, I don't believe you."

"No one is here!"

Valen's left temple began to tick, quickening with her denials. "How dare you continue with this charade? Where is he?"

"Where is who? I'm alone. I came here last night."

"Stop lying."

"Lying? Valen, you're acting as if I'm having an affair." Thunder roared and lightning struck in the distance as Angel watched Valen's gloved hand snatch her arm.

"That's because you are—with Grace Haze's grandson."

* * * *

Jono crouched down by the edge of the porch, just out of sight and checking to make sure Angel was out of danger.

* * * *

"I know all about your famous Cowboy!" Shock and fear made her speechless.

"How could you have done this to me again? Have you no heart or conscience?"

"I'm sorry."

"Sorry? I've given you everything any woman could want, and you repay me by kissing other men. First you tried to sleep with Jack and now with some cowboy the day of our wedding!"

She no longer felt the inflection of pain he was causing by twisting her arm; the guilt of not being completely honest with Valen from the beginning was a pain felt far deeper. "It's not what you're thinking."

"How can I believe you? How can I believe anything you say?"

"Because it's the truth, let me explain. Please, calm down."

"How can I calm down when you're acting like a whore?" Jono came out from around the house.

"She's no whore."

An ominous silence filled the air as Valen whirled around to face who had spoken to him. Jono was enormous compared to Valen. Adorned only by a pair of blue jeans and a cowboy hat, Jono was three times Valen's size by both height and weight.

Angel gasped. "Jono, please leave us to talk. Don't provoke him."

"I'm not going to provoke anything. I just believe Valen deserves to know how much you've sacrificed, Angel, because you feel so loyal to him for all he's done for you."

"Angel and her loyalties are my concern, not yours!"

"You're wrong; she is my concern. I happen to be in love with her." With devilish, glazed eyes, Valen suddenly lunged forward with his hands striking out.

Jono saw the fists coming out of the corner of one eye and caught both punches instantly in the palms of his hands, stopping the strikes mere inches away from his face.

"Violence won't solve anything between us," Jono attempted to reason as he swung Valen around into a headlock.

Valen wouldn't be contained. He thrashed his elbow upward into Jono's ribs, knocking the air from Jono's lungs and the cowboy hat off his head.

"Jono!" Angel screamed.

But it was too late for warnings. The instant Valen was set free, he kicked Jono backwards hard to the ground, where Jono's head thudded on a small rock.

"Jono!" No answer came; his body was motionless. "Jono!"

Valen slowly turned his head toward the woman crying out and clutching her chest. His eyes were piercing with uncontrollable rage. "Valen, please stop!" She wondered if he was coming for her next. "Let me make sure Jono's alive."

In three strides Valen went to her. He said nothing; he merely picked her up and tossed her over one shoulder to carry her away.

"No, put me down! Valen, Jono's hurt!"

"Put her down, Valen!"

Hearing Jono's voice, Valen threw Angel down, face first into the wet dirt and grass. Valen acted as if he wasn't aware of what he was doing, only that the man he just knocked over wasn't dead.

"Angel! Angel, you all right?"

Valen pivoted to Jono who was struggling to stand with blood flowing down his head from a wound.

"Yes! Run! Run, Jono!"

Jono wouldn't, he wouldn't give Valen an opportunity to hurt her further. As Valen leaped for him, Jono caught him in the air and pinned him down to the ground.

Immediately, Valen tried to retaliate with powerful blows to Jono's midsection with one knee. But this time, no matter how many times Valen thrashed out at him, Jono would not release him.

"Valen, calm down! Please, calm down! I'll go with you!"

"I don't believe that's going to solve anything. That's the worst thing possible for the both of you," Jono said.

"You don't understand, Jono. Valen just needs some time to calm down. After he takes his pills, he'll be rational."

"You're right, I don't understand drug addiction, but I know someone who might."

CHAPTER 30

Embarrassed that she had fainted in front of her brother, LaFordge, Martha said, "I'm not in the mood to be hearing 'I told you so.' Just help me to the car since apparently, I'm overtired."

"Just sleepy, huh? Good, then you rest in Whitefeather's office, because that's where I'm taking you next."

"I will if you and Bear go find Wildshot."

"Forget finding Wildshot." LaFordge felt Martha's weight growing heavier on his arm as he aided his sister outside.

Martha's eyes widened. "Oh no! Get the guns."

"What?"

"Something's wrong!" Martha began hobbling away from him, moving faster than he could believe toward the ranch house. "Get the guns!"

Bear was moving around the porch with a rifle in his hand. Witnessing this, LaFordge immediately rushed toward him.

Trouble was imminent.

* * * *

Angel screamed in horror watching Valen pull a pistol from out of his jacket.

Jono felt the weapon against his ribs. Slowly he rose, giving Valen the freedom to break free from underneath his body that had been pinning Valen's to the ground.

No words were necessary. Valen stood there with a dark intensity in his eyes. Jono understood that Valen was more than willing to commit cold- blooded murder in order to keep Angel.

"Valen, please, calm down!" Angel suddenly stepped in front of Jono, directly in the line of fire. "You don't want to kill Jono. Remember how you felt after Jack's funeral."

"Angel, get out of the way." Jono placed an arm to gently push her to safety.

Angel avoided him by moving closer to the gun. "I'm sorry I didn't tell you about him, but I didn't know what else to do. I was afraid. You know as well as I do Eric Brannett would do anything to keep us together. You and I are his meal ticket to world business connections and money. Then I was afraid that you couldn't handle the truth, and that it would take you over the edge with your pills."

"Angel, get out of the way."

"No, Jono, I love you both. I'm not going to leave Valen when he needs me more. I'm not going to let him kill you either."

"I'd rather Valen shoot me than you!"

"Valen won't shoot anyone once he calms down." Angel took another step toward Valen as his eyes filled with tears. "Isn't that right, Valen? You're nothing like Eric. You have a kind heart."

"I don't want to watch the woman of my dreams walking straight toward her death, Angel!" Jono gasped. "I don't want to lose you."

Angel continued to walk toward Valen, watching the gun foundering in his fingers. "I'm so sorry I hurt you. I never wanted to. I never wanted any of this to happen. I never meant to fall in love with another man. I tried to deny I had feelings for Jono, I tried to walk away from them, but I've never been happier in my life than when I'm with Jono. I've never felt love this strong before. I couldn't even stop thinking about him."

"I don't want to hear this!"

Angel recognized that Valen was beginning to understand. "I love Jono. I want to marry him."

"Don't say you love him again! Stop it!"

Angel moved closer for the last time, her body touching the barrel of the handgun pointed at her chest. "I can't keep hiding from the truth, Valen. I can't keep pretending I have feelings for you that I don't. Jono and I are in love. I love you, too, but I love you more like a longtime friend."

She witnessed Valen's left temple calming its ticking rhythm, his anger turning to grief as his tears began to fall down his quivering cheeks. She knew the threat was over. Valen's outrage had completely turned to sorrow because she had finally spoken the words Valen knew to be true. "I never meant to find a different kind of love."

Others were approaching. From the west, two shadows were stretching out behind the limousine. Inside the porch there were women; Angel could smell their perfume. Then Angel heard a board gently fall from the roof by someone crawling on top. She realized that LaFordge would be insane enough to creep up on a weak, tornado-devastated roof. Suddenly, Bear was walking up behind Valen with a hunting rifle pointed to the back of Valen's head.

"What are you doing, Bear?" Angel gasped.

"Bear, your gun isn't necessary. We're just having a friendly chat." Jono moved with a hand raised in protest. "Tell the family to move back."

From the roof, LaFordge called, "I'm not lowering anything until this man lowers his. I think you're a little too trusting, Angel."

Angel whirled around to find Jono's family. Martha and Tonis were on the porch with revolvers pointed. LaFordge was on the roof with a bird's eye view of Valen through a rifle's scope. Meryl and Nikky were standing behind the limousine. Nikky had a knife in her hand. Meryl had a pitchfork.

"Welcome to the family reunion." Bear smiled at Valen.

Even through Bear's brilliant smile, she saw the determination in his eyes. Bear, too, would not move his weapon until he knew they were safe.

Angel had never seen anything like this. They were all willing to risk being shot by Valen in order to protect their brother and her with any means possible. She couldn't help but be overwhelmed by their family loyalty.

The people of Madison may look at Jono as some kind of hero, a hero made out of a cowboy, but his family loved him dearly. His family was built on devotion and honor. They were all willing to die for him.

"Please, Bear, don't hurt Valen," Angel whispered softly, not realizing Valen had moved his gun and now had a clear shot of Jono over her left shoulder. "Valen doesn't know what he's doing."

As Angel disputed with Bear, Valen's eyes searched the several different kinds of weapons pointed and ready to kill him. His .45 automatic was ready to fire. If his finger pulled the trigger, he'd kill Jono Haze and Angel would no longer believe she was in love with him.

Jono Haze would be dead.

Somehow, Valen thought, murdering the cowboy seemed like a blessing knowing he would have murdered the man who had poisoned her heart against him. Angel was his before Jono Haze came into her life. She was his love, his heart, his life, his! The "Cowboy" couldn't have her because he couldn't live without her!

Living without her would not be living at all.

He had to pull the trigger! Jono Haze had to die, and if a member of his family killed Valen afterwards, so be it. At least he'd be protecting Angel and their relationship to the end. At least he would know Angel wasn't in another man's bed at night.

Jono Haze had to die!

Valen's finger tightened on the trigger. Before the bullet shot from its chamber, a brown horse leaped across the limousine and knocked the weapon out of Valen's hands. The impact sent the bullet to the far right, safely away from human life.

"Wildshot!" Martha praised, glad to see the horse. "Where have you been? I've been looking all over for you!"

Valen could not believe his hand was empty. A hand that had once held Angel close to him, once caressed her alabaster skin, now had failed him so blatantly. Jono Haze was not dead, nor was he.

The gun has vanished.

What would happen now? Angel believed she was in love with Jono Haze. *Bloody hell, if she isn't!* Valen witnessed the love in her eyes when the gun exploded, her scream! Such devastation when she thought he was going to die—all announced her love for the rustic cowboy.

She loved Jono Haze!

Valen's heart tightened in his chest. How could this have happened? How could Angel have fallen in love with some cowboy in Colorado? How could this have happened? Didn't she know how Valen would react? Didn't she know that he couldn't live without her and that she was everything to him?

"I've already seen one man murdered." Valen cursed. But this man was not Jack, was he? Angel never loved Jack. Jack was just someone she met in a club. Jono Haze, she loved. Bloody hell, what could he do to change that? This man wouldn't hit him! He wouldn't take a weapon! Bloody hell, he wanted everyone protecting Jono to withdraw.

Why? Why did Angel have to fall in love with another man? Deep inside Valen knew she never really loved him, but to fall in love with a cowboy who owned a ranch when he owned properties all over the world?

When could this have happened? Wasn't it just last week they were dining over wedding plans—the wedding he had postponed for years.

So many mistakes he'd made! Hell, if he wasn't paying for them every day! The guilt was eating him alive that Jack was murdered because of his love for Angel and to protect the business. This time he raised a hand against her. He never meant to hurt anyone. The world surrounding him went black and the anger built until his rage burst out in wild, irrational, behavior—behavior that only the devil would be proud of.

And because of this insatiable thirst for Angel, he had once set her free. A few days later, Jack was dead as the result.

But now another day had come for Valen to finally face the truth he'd known all along. Angel had never loved him the way a woman loves a man. He could not hide from the truth this time, because now, not only did she know it, she'd admitted her love for another man.

A better man.

"Bear, put the gun down!" Jono wiped the blood from over his mouth as Bear moved closer to Valen. "His gun's gone."

"I will as soon as this man leaves your property."

Leave Angel? Valen would rather die. He pivoted slowly facing Bear and leaned his forehead against the barrel of the rifle. The storm was moving west. Thunder and lightning were far in the distance. Rain beaded down in soft, delicate drops as Angel made her way to Valen's side.

There was something between them, a connection that was not love as love was created to be, but an understanding so deep it was deeper than the darkest oceans.

"Valen, if you let Bear kill you, a part of me will die, too. If you try to hurt Jono again, or any member of his family, I will never be able to forgive you."

Bang! The gun resting against Valen's forehead was suddenly kicked sideways out of Bear's hands. "Sorry, Bear," Jono said, "but I had to make sure you weren't going to kill anyone."

Jono showed Bear that all the family's guns had lowered. "I just wanted to make sure that you were out of danger." Jono patted Bear on the back. Their eyes locked, brother to brother. "Everything's under control now. Come back with me to the porch."

As Bear and Jono began heading toward the ranch house with Meryl and Nikky following, Bear had to remind him, "You're leaving Angel alone with a mad man."

"I know, Bear, I know. I'll keep an eye on him while they talk."

Valen admired Jono, watching him escort his family away to shelter from the rain. Jono was a man who believed the best in people.

Why else would he have let Angel be alone with the likes of him? Jono was a stronger, more confident man. It was no wonder why Angel had fallen in love with him.

Valen winced, torn with the affliction the truth revealed. If only he hadn't wrapped his entire world around her. If only he had never gotten so sick by all the drugs. But he had.

"You love Jono Haze." It was a statement said in horror, not a question.

"Yes." She guiltily witnessed the tears flowing from Valen's eyes and lowered her lashes. "If I could change the way I feel, I would."

He held a gloved finger to her lips. "Shh," he softly whispered, "it is I who has made the mistakes."

"How can you say that after all you have done for me? I owe you my life off the streets!" With all her heart, she wanted to say thank you. "I owe you, my life."

"While I try to take the lives of others and my own, I have done nothing but the worst for you."

Angel could not stand to witness his devastation. It wasn't like Valen to show such open vulnerability. She was accustomed to his sudden temper tantrums, drug abuse and vengeful anger; she did not know how to deal with tears.

"I have made so many mistakes, Principessa. I regret them all. I should have never even raised my voice against you. My parents used to use violence to get control of me, to get respect, and I've turned out worse than the bloody bastards! I use anger to control others and drugs to not have to deal with it."

She raised her hand to his trembling cheeks and began wiping away his tears. "I understood, Valen, I did all along."

She always did. She was his confidant, his friend, no matter what horrible things he had done. Angel had always forgiven him. She had always respected his feelings and that was why he was not blinded by indecision. He wanted to do what was best for her, but could he handle the consequences? Valen knew he couldn't.

"Would you have understood, Principessa, if I had shot Jono?"

"No," Angel answered honestly, pulling her tender hands from his cheeks.

Valen caught them and moved her hands to his chest over his heart. "I know you would not have."

"If that's what you're planning, to still hurt Jono, well, don't bother. I'm going home with you. I don't want any harm to come to him or any member of his family." Angel blinked away her tears, trying to hide the agony leaving Jono would cause. "I don't want anything to happen to you. I must never return to Madison. I know that now."

She loved Jono Haze so much she was willing to walk away to save his life. And she cared so much for him, Valen acknowledged, that she was willing to be his support system for the rest of her life to repay for the debt she felt she owed.

Spasms rocked Valen's chest, caused by the stress of the previous fight. "Valen! Are you all right?"

"You'd rather be his wife, wouldn't you?"

Angel panicked as her hands felt the increasing unsteady rhythm of Valen's heartbeat. "You're getting too upset."

Angel put her hand on his chest. "You're getting too upset."

"Answer the question, would you rather be his wife?"

"It doesn't matter what I want. I can't stay with Jono. It just doesn't matter."

Angel tried to yank her hands from off Valen's chest, but Valen clutched them tighter to his heart and fell to his knees. He was overcome with the very thought of losing her. He was trembling like a wounded child. "It does matter what you want."

She noticed Valen's features were serious with certainly. "Let's discuss this later. We need to get you home to rest."

"I need you to be honest with me, Principessa."

"I've told you, I love him. I'm not going to hurt you anymore."

"Bloody hell, woman, it's about time you did!"

She could not witness the tears streaming down his cheeks, the tears she had caused. "I hate myself for telling you that much. I hate myself for making you cry."

"And I hate myself for never listening to you. How many times did you try to tell me to stop! How many times did you remind me that the pills were killing me? I never listened. I never listened when my memory faded or when I couldn't control my own actions anymore. I never listened. Instead, I continued to use all those pills and you, when I should have been making myself into the man you deserve!"

"Stop it, Valen! Please, stop talking about yourself as if you're worthless."

Valen's heart was locked in a torturous battle with his mind. He was deciding on whether he was going to finally free her. Could he let her live her life with the man she loved, or would he again steal her away, take her in the back of the limousine and never return to Madison? It was unlike him to do the unselfish thing. Valen wondered if it was possible for him to really let her be free.

"I am not worthy of your love."

"Let's go home, Valen. You're talking nonsense."

"Your going anywhere with me is nonsense. You don't love me like a wife. You feel obligated."

"That's not true! I do love you like family. I want to go home with you." How easy it was for Angel to always do selfless acts. If only he could be so generous and free her from his dungeon of sadistic ways. Angel had found love. He should let her go. But could he live without her? Could he ever give up the drugs and become the man that Jono Haze was, the man Angel needed to be completely happy?

Never.

"Be honest with me, Principessa. Would you rather stay in Madison with Jono Haze or come back to New York with me?" She couldn't answer. Tears fell down her cheeks, matching his own.

"Forget me, for once. Forget my addictions or our past. Which would you rather do?"

She halfheartedly whispered, "I'm sorry."

The world around him spun, ripping apart his hardened heart. He knew what was best for her. Yet, knowing the truth was crushing. Nothing would ever be the same, not now, not when Valen knew she would rather be with another man. If he kidnapped her, guilt would drive him mad. Living without her would be living in hell.

She was his center, his best friend, his constant companion.

Valen took her beautiful face in his hands and gazed up at the pretty young woman standing before him. This was his life, to feel her love and care for him. Angel has always appeared so concerned for him. No one else had ever cared so much for him, the maddened beast. Only she found some little hope in his lost soul. Nothing would ever be the same. But one, at least one, of them could spend the rest of their life in happiness. "I want you to stay with Jono Haze. I want you to marry him."

Angel could not believe she had heard Valen correctly. "What?" She searched his eyes and found only unyielding darkness. Valen broke away and darted to the back of the limousine, slipping inside before he changed his mind.

To Angel, this didn't make sense. Valen wouldn't just leave her, free her so easily. She meant too much to him! "Valen, what are you planning?"

"You heard me."

"I don't understand. You're letting me marry another man? You're giving me permission, your blessing?"

"Yes."

"Valen! What are you planning? Are you going to come back and hurt Jono?"

"No."

Angel thought for a moment. "You're not going to hurt yourself? Are you?"

"What happens to me, no longer concerns you. You are in love, Principessa, cherish it, love every minute of it, as I have with you."

Angel saw right through his cool façade and terror scorched her cry. "Valen, there has been enough death. Don't do anything foolish! You need help dealing with all this. Valen!" The limousine door was closing in front of her as she rushed forward to stop it.

The door slammed shut and locked. "Valen, don't hurt yourself, please. Valen!" She began beating upon the locked tilted window with no avail. "No!"

Valen no longer heard her cries. He no longer saw her or felt her attentions. The walls of self-doubt, self-hate were crushing the breath from his lungs and killing his sanity.

He could not handle losing his reason for living. "No," Valen finally answered heavily, "there is no help, Principessa, for me."

CHAPTER 31

Angel was screaming and running after the limousine. Jono's white shirt was clinging to her petite frame. The rain was beating down against her skin.

Suddenly, large male arms wrapped around her, forcing her to stop. She screamed in protest. "Valen's going to kill himself."

LaFordge whirled her around and pointed to Jono jumping on the back of Wildshot. "Come back to the porch, Angel. My brother will take care of him."

"How can Jono help?"

"Never underestimate a Haze, Angel." LaFordge cracked a smile underneath his tall, black cowboy hat.

"Valen hates Jono. He won't listen to anything Jono has to say."

LaFordge laughed. "Do you really think that's going to stop my brother from saving his life?"

* * * *

Valen was pouring a bottle of pills into a dirty gloved hand. This time, he wouldn't engulf his normal few. He would swallow the entire bottle to end his life.

Just as his hands lifted, one holding the pills, one clutching a glass of wine, the limousine jolted, screeching to a stop.

The pills went flying. The glass flew forward to the floor.

"Bloody hell!" Valen sank back into the seat. He glanced forward and witnessed the reason for the sudden stop. Wildshot.

The stallion was standing on his hind legs as the cowboy was dismounting onto the limousine's hood. Valen could see them both through the driver's front window.

"Thanks for stopping," Jono said to the driver.

"No problem." The driver gulped.

Jono gave the driver a friendly nod with a tip of his hat and leaped off the hood of the car to the back of the automobile, where he opened the door.

Valen was slumped on the limousine's couch cushions; depression sank into his soul like lion claws into a helpless lamb.

Jono couldn't help but feel Valen's grief and sympathized. "I never meant to come between you and Angel."

"Go away. Isn't it enough you won her heart?"

"I'm not here to upset you any further. I'm here to…" Jono felt several pills underneath his hand as he leaned against the limousine's floor, bracing himself. Quickly, he gazed across the carpet and saw how many there were. "…talk. How many of these did you take?"

It was no surprise that Valen didn't look at Jono or respond; suspicions and devastations were rife.

"I'm not leaving, Valen, until we do talk."

Hardly receptive, Valen complained. "I have nothing to say to you. I didn't take even one pill because the driver slammed on the brakes! Now, leave me alone."

"I came to help you deal with this."

Valen did not want to postpone his suicidal mission for the man Angel loved. "Then destroy Angel's want for you as her husband."

Jono ignored his remark. "I'd like you to meet a friend of mine, before you do anything rash."

Valen reached for the door handle to cut Jono out of his life forever, but Jono moved in and blocked it from being shut, painfully, with his dislocated shoulder.

"He's an excellent physician. His name is Whitefeather. He's a Native American from these parts who became a doctor. Just outside of Madison, he opened a new medical practice. He has all different kinds of doctors working for him, even some therapists who help get people off drugs or alcohol. Every night they have meetings and have rooms for people to stay long term."

Impatient, Valen erupted. "I don't have time for your nonsense."

"Angel doesn't want anything bad to happen to you." Jono's words trailed as he witnessed the slight curving of Valen's trembling lips. It was obvious to Jono just thinking of Angel brought Valen great pleasure. He could use this to his advantage to have Valen agree to his help. "She cares for you very much."

Valen lowered his head. "I wish I could remember a time when she didn't care."

"Time will mend you."

"How can time heal her broken promises? How can time change the way she feels for you?"

"The way she feels for me doesn't change the way she cares about you, Valen."

"Maybe I liked living a lie and believing I was the only man that could make her happy."

Jono sighed. "You can still make her happy, if you'll come with me and get the help that you need."

"There is no help for me."

"You'd rather give up? You'd rather die and destroy Angel right along with you?" Jono swallowed the lump forming in his throat. "How can you do that to her? Do you think mourning someone you love is easy? It's not. I know because my grandmother just died. It's like a part of you just died right along with them. It's difficult to even know how to live afterwards."

Valen's head slowly turned toward Jono, acknowledging the importance of the message he was trying to get across. Jono was attempting to convince him that if he did commit this suicide, Angel would be the one most hurt.

She had even spoken the words, Valen remembered. "If you die, a part of me will die with you. If you hurt Jono or any member of his family, I could never forgive you."

Angel has been going through hell just as he was. She had even been willing to give up the man she loved just to be where she was needed. Valen hadn't considered how she would feel if he killed himself, her pain—until now, until him.

"Valen, I have to deal with the loss of not seeing my grandmother every day. But she has the luxury of watching over me from heaven."

"I will not, when I die, be going to heaven," Valen said, matter-of-factly.

"I don't know, the Bible says, 'from oppression and violence, He redeems their life and precious is their blood in his sight'," Jono said. "Inside, you're a very good person that just got his heart broken and needs some time to heal. I believe God knows that."

Valen admired the cowboy, admired everything about him: his storybook upbringing, his inner strength and bravery. No other man had ever refused to surrender to him. No other man would ignore death with such courage and be worried, no less, about his attacker. His morals were the highest. His kindness was given when least expected, as if it were nothing.

This man was decent. Valen had never been more positive about leaving Angel with Jono than he was at this very moment, gazing upon Jono's face. He was not a strikingly dashing fellow, but his big blue eyes sparkled with the same caring light that twinkled in Angel's. They were made for each other.

"Valen, what do you think? Will you come with me?"

Valen hated the sight of him, the sound of his caring voice. "I will never go anywhere with the likes of you."

"Come on."

"I'm in a bit of a hurry."

"Oh," Jono gave a radiating pearly smile, "the suicide thing's got a time limit?"

"You're mocking me?" Valen cocked his head.

"No, I just don't see any harm in meeting someone first, that's all."

"And I don't see any reason why I should. I've been to many doctors. Many, and not one has been able to get me off the medicine."

"Whitefeather is different. He's been to many white man's colleges. He combines both Native American and modern medicine to help his patients."

"You want me to go to some kind of Medicine Man?"

Desperate, trying to save Valen's life, Jono attempted another approach. "Well, even if you don't think he'll help, at least go for a few minutes. You do owe me a favor."

"You can't be serious. You're the one who owes me for not dragging Angel back to New York and making her my wife. She was about to leave with me until I was riddled with guilt."

"Love," Jono granted him. "I know. I heard it all. I am blessed with incredible hearing. That was quite a sacrifice, what you did."

Valen gracefully took the handkerchief from his dirty lapel and wiped the tears from his face to be able to scowl at his enemy more thoroughly. Mud spread with every wipe but Valen merely placed it back with his usual gentlemanly grace. "I don't owe you a thing. Bloody hell! Get out of my limousine!"

"You did almost kill me in cold blood," Jono was quick to remind. "I would say you owe me a favor."

"I do owe you for that, but consider our differences paid in full when I take my life."

"No, not even," Jono insisted adamantly. "You owe me! Just meet Whitefeather, stay ten minutes and I'll try to leave you alone afterwards."

"That would be a blessing."

"Yes, considering I'm going to follow you wherever you go and stop you from killing yourself if you don't."

"Why would you try to stop me?" Valen interrogated. "Why are you even trying?"

"I like you."

Valen was flabbergasted. "Why in the bloody hell would you approve of me?"

"Someone's got to believe in you," Jono stated. "Besides, if Angel cares so much for you, so do I."

"How novel." Valen shrugged off the open kindness with sarcasm. "I will go if only to never have to see your face again."

"Deal." Jono raised a hand. "Should I trust you?"

"I never lie."

"No, I suppose you don't, do you." Valen would not accept the proffered handshake; instead, he cursed Jono in every Italian word he could think of under his breath.

CHAPTER 32

As Angel stood in the middle of the dirt road leading to his ranch, Jono was captured by her essence. The sight of her waiting to greet him was thrilling and intoxicating. Her long, raven hair was whipping in the wind. Her cheeks were flushed with worry and love. Oh, she was beautiful. She took his breath away. Without any doubt in his heart and soul, Angel was the only woman he wanted to be his wife.

Jono dismounted with a jump into her alabaster arms. He lifted her, whirling her around and around until they both fell into the grass by the side of the road.

"I was so worried!" Angel gasped. "I thought Valen might try to hurt you again."

"He didn't even try." Jono rolled over onto an elbow, gazing down into her eyes without jealousy, but with understanding.

"Is he going to be okay?"

"Valen is going to be just fine."

"Thank goodness!"

"I took him to see an acquaintance of mine."

"Is this acquaintance a physician?"

"He's a combination of many doctors, psychologist, M.D. and he's also been trained as a Shaman."

"Valen needs someone who can understand the effects of his drug abuse."

"Whitefeather can handle Valen's medical problems." Jono smiled. "When I left, Valen was already talking about being beaten as a child."

Valen had never talked to her about his abuse other than twice, once today, and in a drunken stupor so many years ago. It shocked her that Valen would converse so openly with a stranger. "You're kidding, Valen opened up to him?"

"Valen even admitted that he was thinking about committing suicide now that you have fallen in love with me." Jono lowered his head, his hat shadowing half his face. "Valen even said, 'a better man'."

Angel glanced up into his blue pools and witnessed only true concern for Valen. "I never thought him telling his secrets to someone who could help was ever possible."

"He still only wants what's best for you." Jono admired her and the tiny yellow flowers encircling her delicate hair in the grass. "I like Valen. I really do, Angel."

"Are you sure this Whitefeather can stop Valen from committing suicide?"

"Yes, I'm sure. And even more, Valen's getting the care he needs to put his life back together. Around the clock, Whitefeather and his staff will be watching Valen, making sure he's building the skills to live without drugs and his co-dependence with you."

"I'm not sure he can."

"Oh, Valen can. He's already taken the first step by admitting he's got a problem and agreeing not to kill himself."

"That's wonderful, Jono!" Angel pulled his weight down on top of her into a hug. "How did you do it? How did you do the absolute impossible?"

"Well, it wasn't easy. You should have seen how Valen reacted once he realized it wasn't an office but Whitefeather's small new hospital outside of town."

"It's a miracle Valen accepted help at all."

"I know. I just wouldn't give up, that's all. I feel for Valen, I really do. I can't even imagine what it's like to grow up being abused and having to live with the scars." Jono took a long sigh and released her;

his eyes darkened. "There's something else you ought to know. Valen also told Whitefeather that Eric Brannett murdered a man named Jack and he wants to go to the police with the evidence to put Eric behind bars."

"Then Eric Brannett will go to jail, and we won't be in any danger."

"Whitefeather put together that the guilt of covering up that crime for Eric is what was holding him back from kicking his drug habit. Don't worry anymore." A large, tanned hand cupped her face. "I promise you, Valen is going to be just fine."

"How can I not worry?"

"Trust me." Jono kissed her forehead. "It's best for you to let Valen go for now. You can't help him overcome his addiction. He has to want it for himself. He has to make his own decisions. At least until Whitefeather says to do otherwise."

"You're right. My showing Valen how worried I am would only give him the impression that I still want to be his wife."

Jono disagreed. "You know you do love him, and you don't have to hide your love for Valen from me. Valen's been your best friend for many years. I hope someday he'll be mine, too. But for now, he has to learn to live life without drugs and you as his crutch to lean on. He has to be able to stand on his own two feet."

"Yes, I'm…" Angel was about to add an apology for getting Jono into this mess, but his handsome, rugged features were leaning down toward her. His lips were inches from hers. Her nostrils were suddenly filled with the wild scent of him, leather and man combined into an engulfing musk.

He must have read her mind. "Don't apologize for something or someone that has brought us closer together." Their eyes locked and Jono whispered, "And speaking of that, there was something that Valen wanted me to tell you."

Angel held her breath.

"He said to tell you that if you had to fall in love with someone other than him, he was glad it was me. We have his blessing."

"Really?"

"Yes, Ma'am. He also said to tell you goodbye."

Suddenly she felt free, free to love Jono. Free to fly like the hawks that were circling above them. Her lungs, her breasts, her heart and soul filled with rapid emotions. Valen was freeing her because he no longer needed her.

Never had it felt so wonderful to be in Jono's arms! And so right! They were created to be lovers, man and wife, and now it was all possible. "Tell me this isn't a dream, that Valen's going to be fine and we can still be together."

"It isn't a dream, Angel. We've faced death, storms, Valen's gun, and our love has conquered all."

"It always will." Her lips rose and graced his like fire touching fire.

He moaned as she tantalized his lips. He whispered, "Where's my family?"

"Bear and LaFordge went to take Martha home. Meryl and Tonis went out to get a drink. And Nikky just left, I believe to go pick up her son at your mother's."

"No one tried to stay with you?"

"Meryl and Tonis both tried, but I wouldn't let them."

"Then we're alone?" His voice was husky and hot with desire. His body leaned more upon her, his legs moving against her satin thighs.

"Yes, what shall we do about that?" Her erotic meaning was obvious as her hips moved instinctively to meet his.

His lips swooned down to capture hers, but he stopped. His breath was mingling with hers, their lips a hair apart. "No, not yet!"

"Not yet?"

"I have to ask you something first." Jono suddenly rolled himself off of her body, sat upon one knee and removed his cowboy hat with one hand. "I know, I can't near provide for you like Valen. I can't help your music career or buy you fancy of things. But I will love you forever."

Angel rose on one elbow. She was burning with overwhelming love, happiness and unmistakable desire. Her arm wrapped around his muscular waist and attempted to pull him forward for an anticipated kiss, but he held his ground and would not budge. What he had to ask was the most important question he'd ever ask a woman in his life.

"I'll always try to be a good husband. I'll never be unfaithful or if we argue, it is fine with me, we'll talk things out. You can't help but to be wrong every now and again." Angel burst out laughing and moved inward for the kiss she was longing for.

Again, he dodged her lips, twisting to the side, smiling from ear to ear. "Will you stop for a second, Angel? I'm trying to ask you to be my wife." There was silence for what seemed like a lifetime. Only the hawks above made their cries, and the breeze whistled through the tall grass and flowers around them. Patiently, he waited for her answer.

Tears stung her eyes. "Yes." And she meant it with all her heart.

"Yes?"

"Yes, Jono!" she yelled into the wind. "Yes! Yes! Yes!"

CHAPTER 33

Outside the tiny wooden church in a white and gold trimmed saddle with one string of cans tied to his tail, Wildshot waited. The stallion was grazing by the side of the church. He didn't even try to kick or toss the cans about. It was as if he knew the significance of this day and was proud to be a part of the special occasion.

Never happier in their lives, the wedded couple suddenly emerged from behind the church doors. They were followed by their family: Bear and LaFordge dressed in tuxedoes and cowboy hats with Meryl, Nikky, Tonis and Martha screaming and cheering from behind. They were all so joyous. Even Nikky's young son was tossing rice into the air and laughing at how Wildshot had been decorated with streamers.

"Wait!" Jono heard a familiar voice calling from the crowd.

He lifted Angel in her white dress onto Wildshot's white saddle and turned toward his mother.

She looked so much like him. Her long sandy-blond hair and big blue eyes were dazzling as she took him in her arms. "I just wanted you to know that your father and I are very proud of you. I know your Grandmother would have been so proud, too." She started to cry. Jono hugged her and his sisters came and joined them for a big family embrace.

"A few of us decorated your house while you two were visiting your friend Valen last night, Angel," Tonis announced.

"Really?"

"I hope you two will enjoy it." Tonis let go of Jono and took a step back.

Jono glanced up and saw that all of his sisters had tears in their eyes. "Goodness, you girls look like you're at a funeral with all these tears."

They all released one another, looked at one another and laughed. "We're just so happy for you, that is all." Nikky kissed his cheek. Jono pivoted and noticed Bear and LaFordge talking to Angel.

"Welcome to the family," Bear was saying to her. LaFordge tapped his white cowboy hat.

"Excuse me, boys." Jono moved past them and in an instant was in the saddle behind Angel. She perched his cowboy hat on his head, immediately, even though the brown color clashed with his tuxedo. "We'll see you all in a few days. Just remember, don't stop by for a while." He winked.

"Take care of yourself." Bear patted Jono's arm. "And take care of her."

"With pleasure." The crowd began to throw rice.

"Hey, Wife!" Jono called to Angel.

Angel turned her head, barely hearing his voice over the church bells that were beginning to play Lohengrin's "Wedding March."

"Going home!" And with a yell, "Yaah," Wildshot jumped into a run, heading toward the sun setting in the west. The cans were pounding and crashing against the golden-green earth. Angel's white wedding veil was whipping behind in the wind.

Wild sensations of joy flooded over her. In truth, she did not even care where they were headed, or that the Haze ranch which had been in renovations for months was almost finished. The only thing on her mind was that they were going to live together as a couple, man and wife.

"I'm Mrs. Jono Haze!" She tossed her flowers gleefully into the air without looking back to see who had caught them.

* * * *

The church bells could be heard ringing for a three-mile radius. All over the county, hoots and hollers rang out. Cowboys headin' 'em up and movin' 'em out removed their hats and waved in tribute, acknowledging the wedding of the hero of Madison. One man even cried.

Valen rose from sitting on top of Counsel Hill. He was watching the church from a distance, half grief-stricken, half knowing it was for the best. But either way, he had lost his princess forever.

* * * *

They were both so anxious to begin their blessed wedding night. It didn't take the couple long to reach the open dirt trail at the Haze ranch.

Angel gasped at the beauty of the trees before them as Jono coaxed Wildshot forward. The trees had been decorated with shiny white bells. The house, even from this distance, was breathtaking with three large, white ribbon bows tied around the porch pillars. Even the steps leading to the door were lined with white roses. It all seemed to be a dream for both of them, so perfect; the perfect place to start a lifetime of happiness together as man and wife.

"Welcome home, Angel," Jono said.

Angel knew she would never miss her large apartment in New York. Jono was all she needed in her life to make her feel complete. Jono was her riches, far more rewarding and more exquisite than anything material. She only longed to be his wife always and to give him children someday.

"Whoa." Jono pulled in the reins in front of the steps, jumped off Wildshot, and lifted his big hands to her satin bodice to aid his wife from the saddle. Their eyes locked together, so in love, and he cradled her in his arms instead of bringing her down to the ground.

Without delay, he carried his bride through the blossoming rose garden and kicked the front door to open it. The top half toppled from its hinges. "Don't worry, Angel, I can fix the door tomorrow."

Angel hadn't even noticed part of the door had broken; she was lost in his touch, and in the warmth of his large, muscular body. Her husband was stirring emotions inside her she had never felt before, a paradise on earth she didn't know existed.

Jono tried to open the door by using the doorknob. "The hinge is busted. Now, I can't get it open." Jono retried the doorknob which was blocking their path from getting inside the house. "I'll need to get a screwdriver from the barn unless you want me to kick it all the way down."

"I want you, now. Right here, my husband." She smiled tremulously.

"You want our first time to be on the porch? Don't you want me to carry you over the threshold?"

Her gorgeous gray eyes told him she did not care where they made love, only that they begin what she could no longer wait for.

He lowered his bride down until her small feet gently touched the wooden porch floor. And then her shaking hands went toward his tuxedo vest and she began to undress him. Her alabaster hands feathered his muscles, quivering over his masculinity, feeling the desire burning between them.

"Are you as nervous as I am?" Jono asked as his shirt fell to the porch's wooden floor.

"Yes. Because we're outside or because this is our first time?" She shivered, admiring the man she had just married. Every inch of him was a masterpiece created by God, his size incomparable. His shiny short blondish-brown hair was perfectly cut. His golden necklace was shimmering in the center of his broad tall shoulders. His handsome, rugged features were mesmerizing. He was more than any woman could want. And Jono was hers, all hers!

"I'm not sure." A grin crossed his solid jaw, and his large hands began traveling through her long raven curls to find the back of her wedding dress.

"I think we should just do what's natural," she said.

Jono guided her chin gently back with his hands as he moved his body inward for an unrestrained kiss.

His mouth took hers, melting her clear to the core with such emotional intoxication and unconstrained need. It made her forget all the difficulties they had faced to bring them to this moment.

She clung to him as he turned her flesh to liquid; her blood raced through her veins at unimaginable speeds. Never had she felt this way. Never had she dreamed a kiss could be so wonderful.

Angel's body trembled as her tongue entered between his lips irrepressibly. She would not be denied, not this time; Jono was her husband. She was in his arms, kissing, tasting him, and feeling him relinquish himself with the same rapid abandon.

She wanted him. Her body was ready and she no longer could control her instincts. Together, they lay down, continuing to kiss. His heart was pounding. Her ragged breath was becoming overwhelmed by his beauty and the insatiable need to become a living breathing part of him.

"I love you." Jono breathed the words against her lips.

Her petite, red-tipped fingers responded by trembling as they moved downward to the hem of her wedding dress. His handsome rugged face was still inches from hers, their breaths mixing.

She inched her white dress higher to the center of her gleaming alabaster thighs when his hands caught hers.

"Tell me how you feel about me, Angel."

His frame was a masterpiece of male-defined muscles. His shoulders were as wide as her eyes could see. He had a chiseled thin waist with brown spiffs of hair just around his nipples and stomach.

Jolts of sexual desire fluttered through her. His skin was dark, his hands rough, and he smelled of leather as he moved in between the sanctity of her legs.

"Oh, Jono." She felt his corded length fueled with loving need pressing against the top of her inner thighs. "I love you more than life."

His hands traveled to the bottom of her dress, and he undressed her in one sweep, flinging her garment over her head. Her body was slim and petite with full, rounded breasts that swelled over the confines of a thin, white lace brassiere. Her ivory skin gleamed in the sunset, lush and soft, so soft he noted as his palms began to rub her stomach.

His jaw suddenly tightened, and her arms rose around his thick neck to pull his massive physique further onto her to feel the heat expelling from his body.

He was so willing, eager to please, big, beautiful, loving and ready, ever so ready!

"Angel," he spoke her name in but a whisper. "Sweet, Angel; sweet, Angel." Angel was lost as all-time seemed to cease; any problems of their past were diminished. It was only Jono, only her husband making her burn.

His hands were all over her, rubbing, caressing at her sides. His lips were kissing her face and her neck as he filled her secret place to the full maximum, bordering pleasure with pain.

Her eyes gazed over his handsome face as her cheeks felt swollen from the roughness of his scruffy face and lustful kisses. Angel had never felt so consumed or wanted. He was a loving man, a very passionate man. Jono lowered himself back onto his elbows, cradling her body, loving and treasuring her. His mighty arms wrapped around her.

"I'll love you, forever, Angel," he promised, their eyes locking. Hers were flashing with the fullness of love.

"As I will you."

Her lips were swollen, he noted. Passion was still reddening her cheeks. She was so beautiful, no woman more perfect for him. "I'll always try to be a good husband and make you happy."

Jono never lied. "I know, you will," she said.

He sat up on his knees, straddling her, his body almost as large as a bull's, with his heart as big and as wide as the ocean.

"Would you like to try our bed upstairs next, Husband?"

Jono tossed his hat high into the air; it flew to the porch's roof, bounced off and landed perfectly on the house's doorknob on the half-leaning broken door. "Yes, Ma'am!"

Angel could not see that the hat had landed perfectly on the doorknob six feet away, for she could not drag her eyes away from the "Cowboy" legend of Madison County, the hero of her heart.

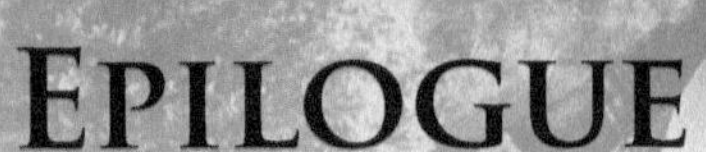

EPILOGUE

Angel watched the long, black limousine coming down the dirt road from her kitchen window. Her heart filled with joy. She had not expected Valen to arrive so soon. She had only received the letter from Whitefeather two days ago.

Dear Mrs. Haze,

Valentino's progress is immeasurable since last time wecon-tacted you. The new EMDR treatments are working well. The past seven months of therapy have given Valen the tools to deal withhis past, the guilt of Jack being murdered and also for his being found incapable of standing trial.

He has been completely drug free for nearly five months.

It is my professional opinion that Valen is now ready to resume his job in New York and begin interacting in society.

Furthermore, I find him fit enough to visit you. It would be of great use to him to converse with you upon a certain subject wehave discussed in our meetings. I trust that you will not mind, hearing the intensity of his extensive progress.

Please call or email me on how the initial meeting went.

Sincerely,

J. Whitefeather M.D.

The limousine parked in front of the blooming sunflower garden and Valen stepped out from the back without waiting for the driver. He was dressed to the hilt in a fine tailored suit and white satin gloves.

He took a long step toward the house then halted instantly upon seeing the beauty with the raven hair staring back at him through the window.

It had been too long. Too long.

A tear rolled down Angel's cheek as Valen continued through the porch and stood in the open doorway. "May I come in, Principessa?" he questioned with grace.

"Of course."

His brown eyes traveled over her, lingering on her face, her neck, until his eyes met hers. There was a distance there, but also a love that had never died; a light shining through. "I hope you don't mind my stopping by before I return to New York."

"I'm glad you did," she admitted, as she began smoothing her sun dress. She suddenly was feeling very conscious of how underdressed she must appear to Valen.

"Don't mind, Principessa. You look amazing," he complimented her, speaking from his heart. "As always."

She blushed and lowered her raven lashes. "You're being very kind."

"I speak the truth."

"I was glad when I heard that you fired Eric Brannett after his arrest. I never liked him even before what happened with Jack. I'm glad he'll be going to prison. Ten years doesn't even seem long enough for Jack's death and for giving you drugs."

"So now you are back in the studio," he said. "I heard the Philmore Agency asked to represent your next album and you signed a new contract with an excellent label."

"Yes, a fresh start with new people. I would love your input. You were the one who discovered me, so I'd like you continuing as my manager. If that is what you would like?"

"I would like nothing more." He smiled. "Although, I will need to distance myself from you for a while until I get over my feelings."

She desperately wanted to run across the wooden floor and wrap her arms around him. But she wasn't sure if she still had the right, or if it would make him feel uncomfortable.

"How is your husband?"

"Fine. He's out in the barn taking care of Sugar."

"Sugar?"

"That's Wildshot's filly. She's absolutely beautiful. You should see her, Valen. She just won first prize in the County Fair."

"As well as your husband winning several prizes for his bull riding." Valen knew. "The 'Cowboy' appears quite a lot in the papers in Colorado, either for his riding or his saving of lives. Although Jono did save one life that never made the papers. Mine."

Angel smiled. "Whitefeather told me that you've made some big accomplishments of your own."

Valen puffed up his chest with pride. "I am completely drug free."

"That's wonderful, Valen."

"I have never felt so good physically or mentally in my life," Valen admitted, "other than missing you."

She wanted to hold him and tell him how proud she was. She wanted to let him know how much she missed talking to him and that she thought of him often.

"Are you as happy as you appear?" Valen's question came out of the blue.

"Yes, I am."

He had to know. "No regrets, then?"

She didn't want to hurt or anger him, so she did not answer.

"Good," he added as if she had admitted 'no.' "Six months ago, I believed I was making the right decision in letting you go, Principessa. I see now that I have made the right decision."

Angel crossed the room and embraced him.

"I wasn't capable of pleasing anyone then, including myself. I wouldn't have been able to make you happy when I was an addict." He lifted one arm around her back, holding her to him tightly.

"Now, I am ready. But it's too late and I never had any right to ask you to wait when I didn't know if I'd ever get well. So, if you ever feel any guilt about falling in love with another man or feel awkward because of it, don't. Please, Principessa, don't. I don't want anything to come between our continuing friendship. I'm through with drugs. I'm through with controlling everyone around me. All I want is what's best for you. That's all I've ever wanted."

"I never loved you the way I love my husband, Valen. But I do love and miss our friendship! Nothing will ever come between us again." She smiled as their eyes locked. "In fact, I have something I want to ask you."

They both heard the loud pounding of cowboy boots coming into the kitchen from the porch. Their heads turned in unison toward the doorframe. Jono, the "Cowboy" legend, was leaning against it. He appeared as he had several months ago to Valen, too big, with the same cowboy hat, same facial stubble, bare-chested with a pair of blue jeans on. He even had the same glimmer in his large blue eyes.

"Valen," Jono greeted matter-of-factly.

"Jono."

"I hear you're doing well."

"I am," Valen confirmed, releasing Angel from the hug, even though there was no hint of jealousy in Jono's voice.

"I've been talking to Whitefeather. He says if you want, you're fit enough to be the Godfather of our child."

Valen stared at him in shock and disbelief for a moment, until the enormity of Jono's words finally sunk in.

"That's what I was about to tell you, Valen." Angel smiled. "I'm two months pregnant and we would like you to be the Godfather to our baby. We want you to be a part of our family."

"But I'm a recovering addict," Valen reminded.

Jono tapped the rim of his cowboy hat. "And you're a member of our family."

Valen swallowed down the lump forming in his throat. He could be the Godfather to Angel's baby. He could have a family! A family where abuse was nonexistent, where love flourished, and holidays were treasured. A Godchild who would depend on him, love him. He would finally have a special place, where he belonged, where he was welcome through good times and bad.

And Jono of all people was asking Valen to join his family, to be a part of his child's life! A man that should hate him, despise him, was opening his home.

Jono raised his hand, offering a handshake. "Will you join us?"

"Are you sure that is what you want? I still have feelings for your wife."

"One of my sisters, Meryl, thinks you're cute. That won't be a problem for long." Jono chuckled. "Once Meryl gets her sights on a man, you might as well put your boots… or dress shoes, that is, under her bed."

Valen laughed. "I'm not even ready to date yet."

"Believe in yourself, Valen." Jono's hand was still hanging in the air, waiting to symbolize a new beginning.

Valen smiled with a glance down at the open hand. Jono returned the smile.

"I do want to be a part of this family. It will be an honor to be your child's Godfather."

Angel sniffed back her tears. "Please stay for Thanksgiving dinner, Valen. We have a lot to be thankful for this year."

Valen's hand rose and shook Jono's firmly. "Yes, we do."

* * * *

Valen joined the Haze family across the elongated table as Jono finished carving the twenty-four-pound Thanksgiving turkey. Valen felt at home. LaFordge, Bear, Martha, Tonis, Jono's parents, Nikky and especially Meryl were making him feel quite welcome.

With blonde hair, big blue eyes and a very fit figure, Meryl's attentions were not bothering Valen at all. In fact, there was something in her eyes when she looked at him.

Suddenly, Jono raised his glass.

Meryl reached over and held Valen's hand as Jono began to say grace.

"We thank you, Lord, for giving us the love that brings this family together. We thank you for this bountiful feast, and for the blessing you have bestowed upon us, this year and in years that have passed. We thank you for watching over our friends who are not able to join us today and for taking care of our beloved who are in heaven now. May you bless and keep, may your love always shine upon us, and grant us everlasting peace."

Around the table, in unison, all replied, "Amen."

ABOUT THE AUTHOR

Michele Wallace Campanelli is an American writer, singer and Florida celebrity. During the early 1990s, Michele was lead singer of the heavy metal band, Black Widow, which was one of the first all-female bands in Florida during the early '90s. After the band, Michele Wallace Campanelli started writing short stories and fiction novels professionally. She has had nine stories appearing on the best-sellers list, including two that reached #1 on the New York Times. Her short stories have been included in over 30 international selling anthologies. She has also penned numerous novels, magazine and newspaper articles in both fiction and non-fiction published by Whiskey Creek Press, Simon & Schuster, Chronicle Books, Fireside Books, Fictionwise, Florida Today Newspaper, Woman's World Magazine, Adamsmedia, McGraw-Hill, Multnomah Books, Red Rock Press, HCI and America House Publishing. Over 57 million people have read her written works internationally. In 1998, Michele wed Louis V. Campanelli III at St. Mark's UMC in Indialantic, Florida. When Michele isn't writing, she is CEO of Regal Entertainment Services LLC which performs concerts around Florida. She is a professional singer, writer and actor. As a devoted Christian, she uses her talents to glorify God and bring joy to others through music and her books.